Mystery

Widows Wear Weeds

Widows Wear Weeds

A. A. Fair
(ERLE STANLEY GARDNER)

William Morrow & Company, Inc.
New York, 1966

M

213167

Chapter 1

It had been a tough morning and there were no signs of a letup during the first part of the afternoon.

I had been working on a complicated accident insurance case and had been out on the firing line almost constantly for a full week. Now I was trying to get my reports caught up. There wasn't time to dictate them in shorthand, so Elsie Brand, my secretary, had been taking them direct on the typewriter, doing a good job, but nevertheless under the terrific strain which comes when even the most competent secretary is making an original and four copies from direct dictation.

At three o'clock we had wrapped it up and I drew a sigh of relief. Our client was coming in at five o'clock that night to get the report from Bertha Cool, my partner in the detective agency.

Bertha Cool, built like a sack of cement, had that hard-boiled exterior which appealed to clients. I did the legwork. Bertha ran the office, fixed the fees, for the most part, and handled investments.

Elsie racheted the last sheet of paper out of the typewriter. "That's the end of that case. With the information you've uncovered, the insurance company will settle for peanuts. They'll be tickled to death."

I nodded. "We'll let Bertha study the reports before the client comes in so she'll know how to fix the fee. Let's take a coffee break."

"I could use about two cups of coffee right now," Elsie admitted.

I gathered up the reports, took them into Bertha Cool's private office.

Bertha Cool was seated in her creaky swivel chair behind the battle-scarred desk.

"You got it?" she asked.

"I've got it."

Her diamond rings flashed cold fire as she reached to grasp the reports.

"That's a hell of a lot of reading to do between now and five o'clock," she said.

"It buttons up the case," I told her.

"In our favor?"

"In our client's favor."

Bertha grunted, picked up her reading glasses from the top of the desk, adjusted them, and started reading.

"Sit down."

"No, thanks, I'm bushed. Elsie and I are going out for a coffee break."

Bertha didn't look up from the reading. "You and Elsie!" she snorted.

"That's right," I told her, and walked out.

Elsie was waiting for me. "Okay?"

"Okay."

"Does she know we're going?"

"Yes."

"What did she say?"

I grinned at her.

"Printable?" she asked.

"Printable," I said.

"That's a relief," Elsie said.

"Bertha was preoccupied," I told her. "She had started reading. It cramped her verbal style. Come on, let's go."

We went down to the coffee shop in the building and found a booth.

"A big pot of coffee," I said, "some toasted crackers, and a double order of Camembert cheese."

"Donald," Elsie protested, "my figure!"

"Wonderful!" I told her.

The waitress hurried off with the order. I settled back and unwound. I had been pretty well keyed up, reading my notes, translating them into the type of report a client could understand, keeping pace with Elsie's fingers on the keyboard, trying to space the dictation so there weren't any pauses yet she didn't have to drive herself in order to keep up.

The waitress brought the coffee. "I thought you'd like this right away," she said. "The cheese will be along in a few moments. We're toasting the crackers."

"Great," I told her.

The man who came in stood aimlessly looking around for a moment, seemed to be trying to locate someone rather than selecting a place where he wanted to eat.

His eye drifted over to our booth, paused, came back again, then hastily looked away.

The man sat down at a table in the center of the room —a table from which he could see our booth.

I said to Elsie, "Don't look now, but I think we're being tailed."

"Good heavens, why?" she asked.

"I don't know," I said.

"The man who just came in?"

"Yes."

"What in the world would *he* want?"

"Well," I said, "he'll probably order coffee and dough-nuts. But what he really came in here for was because someone had told him we were here and he wanted to check."

"Someone who came to the office looking for you, and Bertha told him you were down here?"

"I doubt it," I said. "It could be, but he looks as though he had money; and if a potential client came in and looked as though he had money, Bertha would have said, 'Sit right down there. I'll have him for you within two minutes.' With that, Bertha would have dispatched one of the typists down here telling us to get up there in a hurry."

Elsie smiled. "You've been with Bertha long enough so you not only know what she'd say, but you have the knack of making your voice sound almost like hers."

"Heaven forbid," I said.

Our cheese came and we had the hot toasted crackers and cheese. The man at the table had coffee and a chocolate-covered doughnut.

"It makes me nervous," Elsie said, "like—I feel like a fish in an aquarium with kids staring at me."

Abruptly the man pushed back his chair.

"Here it comes," I said.

"You mean he's coming over?"

"I think so. He's just made up his mind."

The man got up from his chair, marched directly over to our booth.

"Donald Lam?" he asked.

I nodded.

"I thought I recognized you."

"I don't think I know you," I told him.

"I'm quite certain you don't. I'm Nicholas Baffin."

I didn't offer to get up or to shake hands. I simply nodded and said, "How are you, Mr. Baffin?"

He looked expectantly at Elsie.

She didn't say anything and I didn't either.

He said, "It is of some importance that I talk with you, Mr. Lam."

"I'll be up in the office within ten minutes," I told him. "You may see me there."

"As it happens, I would like to get to know you first. . . . That is, I would like to talk informally with you. . . . Could I bring my coffee over here and have a brief few minutes with you? It's on a matter of business."

I hesitated, looked at Elsie, sighed, said, "All right. It's during business hours. It'll cost you money."

"I expect to pay for your time—to pay well."

I said, "This is Elsie Brand, my secretary. Bring your coffee over."

He hurried back to the table and came over with his coffee cup and the uneaten half of his doughnut.

I made room for him to sit down.

He said, "Your firm is Cool and Lam?"

"That's right."

"You've done some rather spectacular work as private investigators."

"We've handled some interesting cases."

"With, I understand, great satisfaction to the clients."

"And your interest in that?" I inquired.

He laughed nervously and said, "I have a very delicate matter and I hardly know just how to bring it up."

"A woman?" I asked.

"A woman is involved, yes."

"In what way?" I asked.

"How many ways are there?" he countered.

"Quite a few," I said. "Blackmail, alimony, paternity suits, broken hearts, and just plain sex."

He glanced apprehensively at Elsie.

"She's been my secretary for some time," I said.

"I guess this is just plain sex," he blurted, "—as far as the woman angle is concerned."

"There's another angle?"

"Yes."

"What?"

"Blackmail."

"By the woman?"

"No."

"You sure?"

"Yes."

"Go on," I said.

"How," he asked, "do you deal with a blackmailer?"

I said, "You lay a trap, get a tape recording of the blackmail offer, scare the living hell out of the guy, and then go free.

"Sometimes you go to the police, confide in the police what it's all about. The police lay a trap for the blackmailer; and if you've got political pull, everybody plays ball."

"Isn't there another way?"

"Sure," I said.

"What?" he asked.

"Murder."

"There's still another way," he said.

"What's that?"

"The pay-off."

I shook my head. "That's like trying to get out of deep water by walking away from the shore."

"In this case," he said, "unfortunately, it's the *only* way."

"A pay-off?"

"Yes."

I shook my head. "It won't work."

He finished his coffee, pushed the coffee cup away, said, "Do you know Sergeant Frank Sellers?"

"Very well," I told him.

"And I believe he knows your partner, Bertha Cool?"

"Yes."

"I understand he and Bertha Cool get along very well together."

"They talk the same language."

"And you?"

I said, "Sellers and I get along. I've been on the inside of two or three cases where I've given him a chance to come out on top smelling like a rose. In other words, we've been good friends at the finish, but prior to that time there's been what you might call an element of suspicion. . . . Sergeant Sellers thinks I am willing to cut corners once in a while."

"He thinks you're smart?"

"Too smart."

Baffin nodded. "That's what I'd heard," he said.

"All right," I told him, "you've taken up time. You've had a lot of fun asking questions. You want to ask any more?"

"Yes."

"Put down fifty bucks," I told him.

He laughed and said, "I had heard Bertha Cool was the manager of the outfit."

"Bertha," I said, "would have had the fifty dollars out of you before you brought the coffee over."

He took a leather folder from his pocket, opened it, reached in and pulled out a fifty-dollar bill. I took it and said, "Elsie will give you a receipt when we go back to the office."

He said, "I run Baffin's Grill."

"I've heard of the place," I told him. "It's supposed to be pretty high class."

"It's *very* high class. I pay my chef *big* money. He has a couple of assistants who get more than the average chef."

I didn't say anything.

"Do you suppose," he went on, "that it could be arranged so that . . . well, so that you and your partner, Mrs. Cool, and Sergeant Sellers could be there for dinner tomorrow night?"

I shook my head.

"Why?"

"It would take manipulation; and any time you try to manipulate Frank Sellers, you're trying to push a granite rock while you have a sore shoulder."

"Everything would, of course, be on the house," he said. "Champagne, steaks, the works."

"That," I told him, "would appeal to Bertha but it

might not to Sergeant Sellers. He'd want to know what he was doing there."

"It must be handled in such a way that he'd never know."

"Just what *would* he be doing?" I asked.

"Lending a certain touch of atmosphere."

"I'd want to know a lot more about it."

"You'd know *all* about it."

I said, "We've just cleaned up a case. It has an angle in it that might appeal to the police. Sergeant Sellers would probably welcome the information. It possibly *could* be given to him over a dinner table."

His face lit up. "Bertha Cool could invite him to dinner with the understanding that it was her dinner?"

I laughed at him. "If Bertha offered to spend the price of a dinner on Frank Sellers, he'd call a psychiatrist."

"*You* could invite him, then."

"It *might* work."

"Bertha is close?" he asked.

"Tight," I said. "A dollar coming in looks like a dinner plate. A dollar going out looks like a drain cover."

"I see," he said thoughtfully.

"Perhaps," I told him, "you'd better tell me just what you want, and since people have just come into the booth behind us, you'd better keep your voice low."

He leaned toward me and said, "I am aware of that. I noticed your secretary's eyes moving as she sized up someone behind us. I felt it was a couple coming into the other booth."

"Anyhow," I told him, "this is a hell of a place to talk business."

"I'm not talking business. I'm talking preliminaries. They're important."

"Why?"

"I'm being blackmailed," he said.

I nodded. "You told me that."

"The blackmailer wants ten thousand bucks."

"This is the first bite?" I asked.

He nodded. "He assures me this is a one-bite deal."

"I know," I said. "They all say that."

"For reasons which I can't go into at the moment, I have got to pay off."

I shook my head.

"It's the only way I can protect the woman in the case. I've got to do it."

"When are you going to pay off?"

"Tonight."

I said, "Don't be silly! You pay ten thousand dollars tonight and within six months you'll pay twenty thousand. And you'll keep on paying until you're out of the restaurant business. Every time it'll be some excuse. They have it down to a science. They'll say they intended to play fair with you, but there's this matter that came up where they themselves are being blackmailed and they've simply got to raise money. You're the only source they have.

"Then he'll tell you that he's sick of the whole rotten rat race; that he wants to go to South America and get into business; that he has an opportunity to go in with a partner; that, this time, it won't be a payment, it will be a loan—an absolutely gilt-edged loan; that you can count on his repayment. He'll even give you a promissory note."

Baffin looked worried.

"Still going to pay off?" I asked after a short silence.

"Still going to pay off this once," he said. "I have to do it."

"Why talk to me?"

"Because," he said, "I want you to make the pay-off."

"What good will that do? Ten thousand bucks is ten thousand bucks; and a blackmailer is a blackmailer."

"You don't get it. You make the pay-off. Then tomorrow night you, your partner, Mrs. Cool, and Sergeant Frank Sellers will be dining at my restaurant. People will see you. One of the people who sees you will be the columnist, Colin Ellis. He will mention in his column, 'Goings On About Town,' that Cool and Lam were hosting a party at Baffin's Grill—a convivial foursome with steaks and champagne. Everybody seemed to be in a happy mood, as though perhaps celebrating a business matter brought to a satisfactory conclusion."

"A foursome?" I asked.

He nodded his head toward Elsie.

"All of this," I said, "would take a lot of doing."

"You have the reputation of being successful," he said. "In fact, in inner circles, you're getting *quite* a reputation."

"What about the outer circles?" I asked.

"Things percolate."

"And what about the blackmail tonight?"

He said, "We leave here, go to your office, and you get instructions."

I shook my head.

"No?"

"No," I said. "Elsie and I go back to the office. You come in and contact Bertha Cool. You tell her your story. She fixes the fee."

"How do I explain the fifty dollars I've already paid?"

"You don't," I said, and slid the fifty dollars back across the table.

"I'm afraid I don't understand," he said, reluctantly taking the fifty.

"You will," I told him. "That fifty was simply to shut you up in case you were one of these fellows who thinks he can get free information by getting a professional man away from his office. Those kinds of people are everywhere. Doctors avoid social parties because they have to make a diagnosis over the bridge table. Lawyers go out to a dinner party and some guy in a black tie sidles up alongside and says, 'Say, Counselor, I've got one for you. This is a funny case that happened to a friend of mine. Let me tell you about it and see what you think.' "

"I never did do business that way," he said.

"I couldn't be sure," I told him, "until I had made sure."

"And you made sure by asking for fifty?"

"That's right."

"What would Mrs. Cool do if she knew that you had given a client back fifty dollars?"

"Bertha Cool," I said, "would have kittens."

"It could be, you know, that I wouldn't even show up at the office."

"Could be," I said, looking at my watch. "Better give us ten minutes to get up there and get oriented. Then you come in and ask for Bertha Cool. Tell her your problem."

"I don't want her to know all of it."

"Even I don't know all of it," I said. "You're holding out."

"There are some things I have to hold out."

"Holding out on Bertha," I said, "is a little different from holding out on me. But cold, hard cash makes Bertha very amiable."

"Quite friendly?" he asked.

"Purrs like a cat," I assured him.

"How much cash?"

"More than you had contemplated paying."

"It's a relatively simple matter," he said, "just passing over ten thousand dollars."

"Tell that to Bertha," I told him.

He hesitated a moment, said, "Thank you, Mr. Lam," and took his coffee cup and the empty doughnut plate back to the table in the center of the room, seated himself and sipped the dregs of the cold coffee.

I nodded to Elsie. "Let's go," I told her. "Bertha will be keeping track of the time. She'll know what time it was when we went out, and she'll make it her business to know the time it is when we get back."

"And you aren't going to tell her about Baffin?"

"Don't be silly," I said. "A partnership is a two-way street."

We went back to the office.

The phone rang.

Bertha was on the line. She said, "You must have had a dozen cups of coffee."

I said into the telephone, "I was talking business."

"With Elsie?" Bertha asked sarcastically.

"With a man by the name of Baffin who is going to come to see you in about five minutes. You're not to let him know that I've tipped you off. He owns Baffin's Grill. He has money. He's in a jam. He wants us."

"How deep is he in?"

I said, "That's in your department, Bertha. I'm too soft-boiled; I was afraid to try and find out. I told him you made all the business and financial arrangements. I suggested he'd better come in about ten minutes after we returned to the office and not let on that he had met me."

Bertha's voice lost its chill. "Donald," she said, "you're learning. You really *are* learning."

Chapter 2

It was around four o'clock when my phone rang and Elsie Brand said, "Bertha wants to know if you can come in."

I winked at Elsie, patted her shoulder as I walked by, went from my private office through the general offices and through the door marked: B. COOL—*Private*.

Nicholas Baffin was sitting there looking as though he had been washed in hot water without starch.

Bertha said, "This is Nicholas Baffin. He owns Baffin's Grill. Donald Lam, my partner."

I simply bowed my head.

Bertha opened a drawer in her desk, took out ten fifty-dollar bills, said, "Mr. Baffin has given us a retainer of five hundred dollars. He wants your services tonight."

"Doing what?" I asked Baffin.

"Paying off a blackmailer," he said.

"That doesn't usually work," I told him.

"It has to work this time," Bertha said. Then she turned to Baffin and went on, "Donald will make it work. He's a brainy bastard. Now, I've got some work to do before we close up so you two get out of here and make your plans and I'll check with Donald in the morning."

Baffin said, "If everything goes right, and I'm satisfied it will, I'd like to have a little celebration dinner tomorrow night at my Grill—tenderloin steaks, stuffed baked potatoes, champagne, the works. All on the house, of course."

Bertha blinked her eyes at me.

"If you could make it a foursome," Baffin said, "I'd have a table reserved."

"A foursome?" Bertha echoed.

Baffin nodded. "I know that Donald Lam could scare up a date who would like to go with him, and you, Mrs. Cool—I think you were in my place about six months ago with an officer, weren't you?"

"An officer?" Bertha asked.

"Sergeant Frank Sellers."

"Oh," Bertha said, "we were working on a case that Sellers was interested in, and he bought me a dinner and gave me a third degree all at the same time."

"Tell him you're returning the compliment," Baffin said.

I could see the idea appealed to Bertha.

"He's done us a couple of good turns," she said, and then added thoughtfully, "but I'd have to tell him that we'd done a job for you and that you were giving us a complimentary dinner."

"Why, certainly," Baffin said, "that's what I expected you to do."

"Well, we'll see how things turn out by tomorrow," Bertha said, and nodded to me. "You go with Mr. Baffin, Donald; and when you deal with that blackmailer, put the fear of God into him."

"Blackmailers are tricky," I told her. "That's why they get into the racket in the first place."

"And they're sneaky," Bertha said, "and they don't stand up and fight. They put bugs in bedrooms and snoop and cower and whimper when someone stands up to them."

Baffin looked me over critically and said, "You don't seem to be overburdened with beef, Lam. Do you think you can make a blackmailer cower and whimper?"

"He's overburdened with brains," Bertha said before I could answer the question. "And you watch your blackmailer cower and whimper."

Baffin got up. "Shall we go and make plans, Lam?"

"Let's go," I said.

I led the way back into my private office. Baffin sat down and whistled. "Five hundred smackers!" he said. "There's nothing modest about your partner, Lam."

"I never said there was."

"Well," Baffin said, "as you may have surmised, I'm

doing this not for myself but to protect the good name of a woman."

"And what's the good name you're protecting?"

"I'd rather you didn't know her except by her first name," Baffin said. "The first name is Connie. We'll go to see her at seven o'clock tonight, if you don't mind."

"When do we meet the blackmailer?"

"Eight."

"How much do we pay him?"

"Ten grand."

"Why do we have to see the girl?"

"Because," Baffin said, "she's putting up the money. It wouldn't be convenient for me to put it up right now and, besides, it's her party."

"Seven o'clock," I said. "Where do we meet?"

"I'll pick you up at the entrance to the building. I'll have my sports car."

"Seven on the dot," I told him. "I don't like to stand around waiting."

"Everything is going to be done on the dot," he said. "We're working on a split-second schedule."

"Okay," I told him. "See you at seven, and remember it's the girl's party."

Chapter 3

Baffin met me right on the dot of seven o'clock. He was driving a high-priced sports car.

He pulled in to the curb and opened the door, and as I climbed in beside him and fastened the seat belt, he said, "Now, you understand I'm doing this for the woman in the case."

"That's what you've told me."

"Only for her."

I didn't say anything.

"Otherwise, I'd have told the blackmailer to go jump in the lake."

"You're married?" I asked abruptly.

"What does that have to do with it?"

"In blackmail, it has a great deal to do with it."

"Yes," he said shortly, "I'm married."

We drove in silence for a minute or two.

"My wife," Baffin went on, "has developed into a cold-blooded, mercenary gold digger."

"Any chance of a split-up?" I asked.

"All the chance in the world."

"Then you don't think she's back of any of this?"

He shook his head.

"Why not?"

"Because I know the setup," he said. "My wife and I have been trying to get the goods on each other for the last seven or eight months. She's known that I was playing around—in fact, she made damn certain that I *would* be playing around. She moved into the guest bedroom. She keeps the door locked. I seldom even see her any more. When I do see her, she's cold as ice. And she's been hiring private detectives."

"But she hasn't got the goods on you?"

He grinned and said, "I'll tell you something confidentially, Lam. I'm a pretty damn smart hombre."

"How come?" I asked.

"I knew I was being tailed," he said. "I got the license numbers of the cars, traced them to the detective agency she'd employed and found out she'd hired two detectives in eight-hour shifts.

"Not only could I ditch the shadows whenever I wanted to, but I had eight free hours every day, because she was too tight to order the shadows in three shifts."

"Then this blackmailer could sell out to her?" I asked.

"He's not going to sell out to anyone," Baffin said. "We're going to pay this blackmailer off and be done with him."

"Well," I said, "it's always advisable to have an optimistic approach toward life. It seems the blackmailer is letting you off pretty easy for ten grand, under the circumstances."

"He's not letting *me* off," Baffin said. "It's Connie."

"You mean the blackmailer doesn't know you're married?"

"I don't think that angle has occurred to him at all. He's putting the bite on Connie."

"Then when he gets done with her, he'll put the bite on you."

"That's why I have you along."

"I can't accomplish the impossible," I said.

"It isn't impossible," he told me. "You know the ropes in these things. I don't. You're going to have to put the fear of God into this guy. Frighten him with one hand; pat him with the other; put ten thousand bucks in his pocket, then kick him in the seat of the pants; and *get the evidence*."

"Just what is the evidence?" I asked.

"Photographs."

"Intimacies?" I asked.

"Leaving a motel together and a registration card in my handwriting."

"And the registration card?"

"Nicholas Baffin and wife."

"The address?"

"The address is okay but he's got the license number of my car."

"Lots of people," I pointed out, "register as Mr. and Mrs. John Smith. Just in case there should be a next time."

"I know they do, but I was putting across a business deal. I had to be available for a phone call and—what the hell, I made certain I wasn't being shadowed that night."

"But you're certain you've been shadowed lately?"

"As I said, my wife has had a detective agency on my trail for over a month. She had me tailed seven nights a week, four o'clock in the afternoon to midnight; midnight to eight o'clock the next morning. Fifty-five dollars an operative, plus expenses—a hundred and ten dollars a day. She threw in the sponge and quit it a couple of weeks ago after she'd run up a shadowing bill of over two thousand bucks."

"Then you knew about it?"

"Sure. I knew *all* about it."

"What did you do?"

"I sat tight."

"For the whole period of time?"

He grinned. "Hell, no. If she'd had the detectives on a twenty-four-hour-a-day basis, she'd have hit pay dirt; but she felt I'd be conventional and only wander away after four in the afternoon and before eight the next morning."

"I see," I said.

"There's plenty you *don't* see," Baffin said. "Just concern yourself with what we have to do tonight, but make it good."

"All right," I told him, "I'll try and make it good. We're on our way to see Connie now?"

"That's right."

"And Connie is going to give me the money?"

"Yes."

"If it's any of my business, why didn't Connie simply give you the ten grand and let you give it to the blackmailer?"

"Because," he said, "this is Connie's party, and I'm going to put on an act."

"What kind of an act?"

"I'm going to help you put the fear of God in this blackmailer."

I said, "I'm not certain that I like this business. I either like to be in charge or be relieved of all responsibility. I don't want to work on a basis of divided authority."

Baffin said, "You've got five hundred bucks for an evening's work. You do your job; I'll do mine."

We turned down Grand Avenue and came to a stop in front of the Monarch Grand Apartments.

Baffin turned to me and said, "Now, you may recognize Connie. If you do, don't let on."

"You mean we've met before?"

"I'll put it this way; you may have seen her some-where."

"On the screen?" I asked. "On television?"

"Somewhere," he said, and parked the car.

"You're sure you want me to go up with you?"

"Absolutely certain. That's the way it has to be. She gives the money to you; you pay it to the blackmailer."

Baffin looked at his watch. I looked at mine. I realized then that it was the second time in ten minutes Baffin had looked at the time.

We took an elevator up to the fourth floor. Baffin led the way and tapped on a door.

The door was immediately opened by one of the most beautiful women I had seen for months, either on or off the screen.

"Hello," Baffin said.

"Hello," she said.

Baffin said, "This is a detective."

"Come in," she invited.

It was a nice, impersonal apartment.

"This is Connie," Baffin said.

"How do you do," I said.

"Won't you sit down," she invited. "How about a drink?"

Baffin said hastily, "I don't think we'd better have any." He looked at his watch again, said, "We're all set, Connie."

"The detective understands what he's to do?"

"Yes," Baffin said.

"No," I said.

She looked from one to the other of us.

I said, "I've been told that I'm supposed to pay ten thousand dollars. What do I get in return?"

"You tell him, Connie," Baffin said.

"You get a picture, a photograph taken at the Rest-abit Motel on the sixth of this month at about nine-thirty in the morning. The photograph shows Nicholas Baffin and myself. He is just helping me into the car. Our faces are very plainly recognizable. Moreover, the license plate on his car is legible.

"In addition to that there is a card of registration, Nicholas Baffin and wife, stating Mr. Baffin registered in at the Restabit Motel on the evening of the fifth at about ten-thirty o'clock."

"The original registration card or a photographic copy?" I asked.

"The original registration card."

"How did the blackmailer get that?"

"Heaven knows!"

"How did he get the picture?"

"Very, very simple," she said. "He had his car parked in the parking lot. When Nicholas brought out the baggage, this man warmed up his motor. When Nicholas put one of the suitcases in the trunk, then came around to help me into the car, this blackmailer shot his car out into the driveway.

"There wasn't room enough for him to get by. I motioned with my hand for him to go back. Nicholas turned and shouted at him, 'What's your hurry, buddy?' —or something of that sort.

"The man looked a little drunk, a little groggy. He sat there and grinned. We didn't see any camera. It must have been concealed somewhere in the automobile."

"You've seen a print of the picture?"

"Oh, yes."

"And what about the registration card?"

"We've seen a photographic copy of the registration card."

I said, "You understand that photographic copies are a dime a dozen. A man can make a thousand copies. When he has the original card, he can make a hundred negatives. I can demand that he surrender the prints and the negative. He'll surrender the prints, a negative and an original card.

"The card he may not be able to duplicate but he undoubtedly has taken photographic copies of it. In fact, we know he has because you folks saw a photographic copy.

"I can buy negatives and prints and destroy them, and a week from today some entirely different person may show up with a story about being a photographic technician; that the blackmailer called on him to make some duplicate photographic copies; that he did so without realizing he'd struck pay dirt until he recognized the people or until he had looked up the license number on the automobile or some such line of malarkey, and then you find yourself dealing with a brand-new blackmailer and a brand-new demand."

"That's why we have you," she said.

"To do what?"

"To see that this doesn't happen."

"You expect a great deal," I said.

"We paid a great deal," Baffin said.

"Now, this was on the morning of the sixth?" I asked.

"Yes."

"Just a week ago," I said. "Today's Monday, the thirteenth."

"That's right."

"And the registration was on the fifth?"

"Yes."

Baffin looked at his watch. "I think Donald understands everything, Connie."

"Oh, your name is Donald, is it?" Connie asked.

I nodded.

"It's a pretty name. It sounds honest and sort of competent."

She looked me over.

Baffin fidgeted impatiently.

She got up, walked over to a door which evidently led to a bedroom, said, "I'll only be a minute."

She was less than thirty seconds. She came back with a bundle of currency and handed it to me.

I counted it. There were one hundred hundred-dollar bills in the package.

"You want a receipt for this?" I asked.

She laughed and her laugh was musical. "Heavens, no! All I want is to be out of it."

"Ten thousand bucks is a lot of dough," I said.

"I know it," she said, "but it doesn't mean as much to me as you think it does. This came from the studio."

"What studio?" I asked.

"Don't tell him," Baffin said.

She said, "Why not, Nick?"

"He hasn't recognized you," Baffin said.

She smiled at me and said, "I guess I shouldn't have said that."

Baffin said, "It's time to go, Donald."

I got up.

Connie gave me her hand. "Good luck," she said.

"I'll probably need it," I told her.

Baffin opened the door and she ushered us out into the corridor. Four minutes later we were in Baffin's sports car.

"Now, you've got that dough all right?" he asked.

"Don't worry," I told him. "I've got the dough. And now, do you mind if *I* tell *you* something?"

"What?"

I said, "I'm going to keep this dough until I pay it out under conditions that are satisfactory to me."

"That's okay by me."

"I mean nobody's going to take it away from me."

He raised his eyebrows.

"No one," I said. "Particularly, I'm not going to fall for a fake holdup."

"What made you think anything about a fake holdup?"

"I don't know," I said. "It has happened." With that, I opened my brief case which I had left in the automobile, took out the agency's .38-caliber, snub-nosed, blued-steel revolver and settled back with the gun in my lap.

Baffin nodded approvingly. "You're living up to your billing, Lam," he said. "You are, indeed."

I didn't say anything.

We drove rapidly to the Stillmont Hotel. There was a parking lot next to the hotel. It was one of those deals where you take a ticket from an automatic machine as you go in, paying fifty cents in a coin slot.

Baffin drove the car into a vacant space, looked at his watch, said, "Just a minute," got out and walked around the entire parking place. Then he came back, got in the car and sat down.

"What do we do now?" I asked.

"We wait."

"The pay-off is here?"

"Not here—in the hotel."

"What are we waiting for?"

"Until I give the word."

I nestled the snub-nosed gun in my hand and kept the barrel so I could swing it to point at Baffin with a mere flick of my wrist.

Baffin seemed not to notice the gun. He shut off the motor, the lights, settled back, selected a cigarette, lit it with the lighter in the dashboard; then suddenly thought better of it, ground the cigarette out in an ash tray and crushed it down into the receptacle.

I sat there waiting with the gun balanced lightly in my hand.

We waited over ten minutes.

Half a dozen cars came in and parked. A couple of cars went out.

Then a sedan came in, and Baffin suddenly straightened in his seat.

The driver of the sedan parked it about three cars from us, got out, looked at his watch, and walked rapidly toward the hotel.

Baffin waited until the man had left the parking lot, then he said, "Okay, Lam. Here's where you do your stuff."

He held the door open. I held the brief case in my left hand. I put the ten thousand dollars in it and held the revolver concealed by my coat, pointed at Baffin. I kept it in my right hand until we had left the parking lot and were approaching the hotel, then I dropped it into the brief case.

Baffin led the way.

We walked to the desk. Baffin said, "Do you have a Mr. Starman Calvert registered here?"

"Why, yes," the clerk said. "As a matter of fact, Mr.

Calvert just came in. He's in Room seven twenty-one."

"Will you ring him, please?" Baffin asked.

"I'm afraid he's hardly had a chance to get to his room. He just went up in the elevator."

"That's fine," Baffin said. "He's expecting us. We'll go on up."

"I'll have to ring him."

"Sure, go ahead," Baffin said. "Give him time to get to his room. Tell him the party he expected is on its way up."

Baffin led the way to the elevator. We went up to the seventh floor.

A man was waiting at the elevator. I judged him to be about forty. He was slender, short, with a close-cropped gray mustache, and the air of a successful banker. His eyes were a cold blue, the color of a glacier.

He glanced at Baffin, then studied me.

"Thought you'd be in your room," Baffin said.

"I spotted you in the parking lot and waited here for you."

"You couldn't have spotted us," Baffin said.

The man laughed a low-pitched metallic laugh. "Then what am I doing here waiting for you?"

Baffin didn't answer. He said to me, "This is Calvert."

Calvert said to Baffin, "Have you got it?"

Baffin said, "*He* has."

"All right," Calvert said, "let's go to the room."

He led the way down the corridor.

We came to Room 721. Baffin stopped.

Calvert kept on walking.

"Here it is," Baffin said. "Seven twenty-one."

Calvert shook his head and beckoned to us.

We walked on down the corridor to Room 715.

Calvert took a key out of his pocket and unlocked the door.

"What's the idea?" Baffin asked.

"In this business, you have to be cautious," Calvert said, smiling. "I'm registered under my own name in seven twenty-one. I'm registered under another name in seven fifteen. I keep the key in my pocket. In a setup of this kind, one guards himself against all eventualities, house detectives, police, tape recorders and hidden witnesses."

Calvert threw open the door. "Walk right in, gentlemen," he said.

I let Baffin go first. I opened my brief case and held it in my left hand where I could grab the revolver if I had to.

"Right on in," Calvert said.

"After you," I told him.

He hesitated a moment, then laughed and said, "All right, be cagey if you want to. I don't know as I blame you."

He walked in. I followed him and kicked the door shut, then I turned the bolt on the door.

"After all," Calvert said, "we're doing business together. If I had wanted to double-cross you, we wouldn't have got this far. Please be seated, *gentlemen*."

We sat down.

"You have the money?" Calvert asked Baffin for the second time.

"*He* has," Baffin said, again nodding his head toward me.

I took the ten thousand dollars out of the brief case. It made quite a bundle, one hundred hundred-dollar bills.

Calvert's eyes lit up. He reached for the money.

I said, "I believe this is an exchange."

"Oh, pardon me," Calvert said. "I got a little—well, I guess I was jumping the gun a little bit."

He crossed over to a brief desk, took a key from his pocket and unlocked the drawer.

As he did so, I reached swiftly into the brief case and turned on the wire recorder which was concealed inside.

Calvert turned back to face me and opened the Manila envelope he had taken from the drawer.

"Here are three eight-by-ten glossy prints," he said. "They are the only prints that have been made from the negatives."

I studied the prints. They showed the sign, the Restabit Motel, the face of the woman, and Nicholas Baffin's face looking back a bit over his shoulder. The lid of the trunk was up. Baffin had evidently just finished putting one suitcase in the trunk, the other suitcase was on the ground. The license number of his automobile showed very clearly. He was helping Connie into the car.

"Now, here are two negatives," Calvert went on, taking a smaller envelope from inside the big Manila envelope.

The negatives were thirty-five millimeter and they quite evidently had been taken with an expensive camera. They were microscopically sharp.

"The negative which had the better exposure was selected as the one to print," Calvert said. "The other negative hasn't even been printed."

"And these are the only prints that have been made?"

"Aside from the one that was sent to Mr. Baffin," Calvert said.

I nodded.

"Now here," Calvert said, "is the original registration card, Mr. and Mrs. Nicholas Baffin. You'll notice this is the Restabit Motel regular registration card. The date is the fifth of this month. The picture was taken on the morning of the sixth when the parties were checking out."

"Any photographs or photographic copies made of this registration card?" I asked.

"Only the one print we showed Baffin. The negative is in the other envelope. It's a thirty-five-millimeter copy."

"How do we know you're telling the truth?"

He smiled and said, "Obviously there are some areas in which you have to accept ordinary good faith."

"Ordinary good faith doesn't enter into blackmail," I said.

He said, "I don't like that approach. I don't like that

word. I don't appreciate your attitude. This is not black-mail."

"What is it?"

"It is a chance that the parties have to buy up some photographs and some evidence. It's being made very easy for them to do it. There *are* people who would pay far more than ten thousand dollars for this evidence."

"But you're willing to sell it for less?"

"To the proper parties, yes."

"Why?"

"Because I have an urgent, pressing need for ten thousand dollars. The price I have set is dictated by my requirements rather than by the market value of the property."

"All right," I said, "you don't like the word 'black-mail.' You're a darn good photographer. You're in some sort of a jam where you need ten grand. You dislike very much to resort to these methods to get the money, but you are faced with a necessity—a fact."

He nodded. "That expresses it very clearly and concisely."

"All right," I said, "who do you think I am?"

"I assume you are an attorney representing some of the interested parties."

I said, "My professional capacity doesn't need to interest anyone. I am here to make certain that there is one payment, and only one payment."

"You have my word," he muttered.

"Your word of honor?" I asked.

He started to nod, then flushed and said, "Is that meant as sarcasm?"

"It was meant as a question."

"You have my word of honor."

"You have absolutely no intention of doing anything else with this evidence?"

"How can I when I've turned it over to you?"

"There may have been other prints, other negatives."

"There are none."

"So you have absolutely no intention of doing anything else, or approaching anyone else with photographic copies of this?"

"That is correct."

"Then," I said, "you will have no objection if I take certain precautions to see that you don't change your mind, or that someone who may have surreptitiously made extra prints from those negatives doesn't enter into the picture?"

"You may take any precautions you wish," he said.

"All right. First," I told him, "I want to see your driving license."

He hesitated a moment, then took a folder from his pocket, extracted a driver's license and handed it to me.

The name was Starman Calvert.

I crossed over to the desk which was in the room, opened the drawers, found some stationery with the imprint of the hotel on it, took several sheets of the paper back and placed it on the table in front of Calvert.

"What's this for?" he asked.

"This is a receipt for the ten thousand dollars. It's also a guarantee that my client won't be exposed to future embarrassment."

"How can anyone *guarantee* that?"

I said, "Write as I dictate; write it in your handwriting, the date at the top. This is the thirteenth."

"Very well. What do you want me to write?"

I dictated slowly. "I, Starman Calvert, have received ten thousand dollars in cash from Donald Lam. The consideration of this payment is that I am turning over to Lam certain photographs and negatives which I have taken showing a couple loading suitcases in an automobile at the Restabit Motel.

"These pictures were taken on the morning of the sixth. I have turned over to Lam all of the evidence and photographs in my possession. There are no other photographs which have been made from the negatives; there are no other negatives.

"I have turned over a registration card in the Restabit Motel, dated the fifth of this month, and a negative copy of same. That card is the original registration card. No photographic copies have been made of it, except one which was delivered to Lam's client.

"I am badly in need of the sum of ten thousand dollars. Because I have no other way of raising this money, I have resorted to blackmail."

"I don't like that word," Calvert interposed.

"Write it, whether you like it or not," I said.

He flushed. "I don't have to."

"And I don't have to give you ten thousand dollars."

"And I don't have to give you the photographs," he said. "I can sell them elsewhere."

"Go ahead," I invited.

"Look here, I'm trying to be reasonable. I think you can spare my feelings."

"I'm being reasonable," I said. "I am dictating this receipt so that when you sign it you can't come back with more prints, or with some demand by some technician in your studio that more money be paid for prints which he surreptitiously made without your knowledge."

"I told you I didn't like blackmail."

"I told you to write it anyway."

He hesitated for a moment, then, his face flushed with anger, wrote it as I had dictated.

"All right," I said, "now sign it."

He signed it.

"Put down at the bottom 'The number of my driver's license is—' and copy the number of your driver's license."

"Why is that necessary?"

"I want identification."

"You want a lot," he said.

"You've got a lot," I told him.

"I've put up with a lot of indignities since I entered this room," he said.

I shrugged my shoulders and said, "If you have such conscientious scruples and such a sensitive nature, I can imagine that the emergency which caused you to demand ten thousand dollars for the evidence in your possession must be acute. Your need for the money must be extremely great. The emergency must be urgent."

"All right," he said, "you win," and wrote the number of his driving license on the bottom of the page, under his signature.

I pulled an ink pad from the brief case. "Now the fingerprints," I said, "all ten of them."

He jumped up. "I'll be damned if I do!"

I put the ten thousand dollars back in the brief case.

"I've given you enough," he said. "You've got your protection."

I sat there, saying nothing.

He looked at Baffin.

"Can't we dispense with the fingerprints, Donald?" Baffin asked.

"No," I said.

"As the client, I think I am entitled to tell you not to carry this too far."

I sat there, saying nothing.

Calvert flung open a drawer.

Baffin said hastily, "He's got a gun, Calvert."

Calvert slowly closed the drawer.

We three sat there.

At length, Baffin said, "You can do a lot with ten grand. You can leave the country. And Donald is doing this for my protection. He'll give the fingerprints to me, not to the police."

More silence.

Slowly, reluctantly, Calvert touched his fingertips to the pad, then to the paper.

I took the paper, folded it, put it in my pocket, handed him the ten thousand dollars; put the photographs, the negatives and the card back in the Manila envelope and put the envelope in my brief case.

"All right," I said, "now let's see how our wire recording came along."

I took the instrument out of the brief case.

Calvert watched me with startled consternation, then his eyes became angry. He pushed back his chair.

"Sit where you are, Calvert," I said.

"You can't do this to me," he sputtered.

"I've already done it," I told him.

I turned the wire recorder on, and the voices came in strong, loud and clear.

I nodded, shut the wire recorder off, put it back in the brief case. "And remember I have your signed confession, your fingerprints, and the wire recording of what transpired."

I turned to Baffin. "I think that's all we need, Baffin."

Calvert got to his feet. "You don't leave a man very much self-respect, do you?" he said.

Baffin apologized. "I'm sorry, Calvert. I wouldn't have played it this way, but I told Donald I wanted complete protection."

"In dealing with me, you're not dealing with a blackmailer," Calvert said.

I kept quiet, closed the brief case, and opened the door.

I stepped out into the corridor. Baffin followed. Calvert slammed the door shut behind us.

Baffin turned to me and said, "Did you need to be that tough on the guy?"

"You wanted a job done," I said. "I tried to do it. I still don't know if I've done it. What I'm afraid of now is that Calvert will go to your wife's lawyer with duplicate prints."

Baffin's jaw dropped, then he said, "Calvert doesn't even know that I'm married. I tell you it was Connie's party all the way through."

"Let's hope so," I said.

We went down in the elevator, out to Baffin's car.

"You'd better give me the pictures now," Baffin said. "I'll also want the wire recording, the written receipt, and the fingerprints."

I said, "I give the evidence to the one who gave me the money."

"Connie?" he asked increduously.

"Certainly," I said. "All you wanted was to have me give you assurance that she would be safe from further blackmail. I've done the best I could. Connie gave me the money, and Connie gets the evidence. You told me it was her party."

"You can't see her tonight," he said.

"Why not?"

"I—It wouldn't be convenient."

"Then I'll keep this stuff until it is convenient."

"Look here, Lam, you can't do that. I'm your point of contact in this matter."

"If you were the point of contact," I said, "you would have given me the ten grand. But for some reason or other, no one wanted to trust *you* with the ten thousand dollars; therefore, *I'm* not going to trust you with the evidence."

"Lam, you're being utterly, absolutely unreasonable. That wasn't the idea at all."

"Then what was the idea?"

"Connie wanted to protect me. She wanted to get me out of it and keep me out."

"All right," I said, "then I want to protect you. I want to leave you out of it. You can drop me at the office."

Baffin looked at me with glittering hostility. "Why, you son of a bitch," he said.

"Unless, of course, you want to double back to Connie's apartment," I told him.

He drove for a while in silence, then said suddenly, "Now, look here, Lam, you can trust me. I'm your client. I'm the one who came to the office. I'm the one who retained you. It's my five hundred dollars that you have. You're working for me."

I said, "Connie gave me the money. Connie wanted the evidence."

"And I tell you she was trying to protect me."

"If she tells me to turn it over to you, I'll be glad to do so."

Baffin said, "You folks could get into trouble over this, you know."

"In what way?"

"Your license," he said.

"Make all the trouble you want to," I told him. "We're accustomed to it."

He didn't say any more. I could see that he was thinking.

He dropped me off at the entrance to the office. I took the brief case up, put it on the desk, called the Monarch Grand Apartments.

"I'd like to speak with Apartent 405," I said.

"There's no one in Apartment 405," the operator told me.

"I think you're mistaken. I was there earlier this evening and—"

"Oh, Miss Constance Alford rented that apartment this afternoon on a twenty-four-hour basis. This is an apartment hotel, you understand?"

"I understand."

"She was called away unexpectedly. She checked out about an hour ago."

"Thank you," I said and hung up the phone. I took the Manila envelope with the pictures, opened the office safe, put the photographs in a locked compartment to which I had the key, closed and locked the safe.

Chapter 4

I called Elsie Brand at nine o'clock.

"Bertha in, Elsie?" I asked.

"Yes, she's in her office."

"Tearing her hair?"

"No, she seems to be very affable. She even smiled at me when she said good morning."

"She'll be hitting the ceiling within an hour," I said. "I'm going to be out until about ten o'clock doing some legwork. If she asks for me, tell her I'm getting facts on a case."

"Okay. Will do," Elsie said.

I covered the Stillmont Hotel. Starman Calvert had checked out the night before. I covered the various casting agencies. They had a Constance Alford, a Corine

Alford, and a Carmen Alford. None of them was big time. Constance Alford was a relative newcomer. No studio would have advanced a dime to protect her good name.

I went around to the Restabit Motel, showed my credentials, asked if I could look at their registrations on the fifth. There was no registration of a Nicholas Baffin and wife, and they insisted they had all of the original registration cards there in the file.

Of course, they would have insisted that anyway. Short of something of prime importance they wouldn't admit to keeping records which could be purloined by an outsider.

The manager of the place was in a sour mood. A ten-story apartment house was going up across the street. Some of the steel framework was getting in place, and not only was the street all cluttered up with the cars of the steelworkers and trucks bringing in materials, but the place had noisily come to life at eight o'clock in the morning and the motel tenants had been complaining.

I went back to the parking place and mentally reconstructed what had happened, the place where Baffin had his car while he was loading baggage in front of his unit, the place where the blackmailer had parked his car only to move it forward at the crucial instant.

Standing there I could see the tops of beams and a cross girder over the top of the Restabit Motel.

I could gather that the manager wasn't in a very happy position, at least until the construction was finished, and then with the apartments filled he was going to have a crowded street on his hands.

The real estate on which the motel was situated would go up in value. The man who was running the place was working on a lease. The lease expired in eighteen months. The property was going to be too valuable for a motel.

All in all, I could see where *he* was having *his* troubles. He had an excuse to be grouchy. In his place I wouldn't have given anyone the time of day.

I thought of Bertha waiting there in the office, her jaw jutted forward, her teeth clenched in indignation, and realized that when I hit the office *I* was going to have *my* troubles.

I got to the office about ten-thirty.

The girl at the switchboard said, "Bertha said she wanted to see you very first thing when you came in. She wants to see you right away. It's important."

I hesitated a moment, then headed for Bertha's private office.

I braced myself for the shock and opened the door. Bertha was grinning like a Cheshire cat.

"Where the hell have you been?" she asked, but she was still smiling.

"Working," I said. "Legwork."

"What case?"

"Baffin's case."

"You paid the dough over?"

"Yes."

"Got the documents and everything?"

"Yes."

"Think the blackmailer will put another bite on him?"

"No."

"Well," she said, all but purring, "I got hold of Sergeant Frank Sellers. I told him that the agency had done a job for Baffin's Grill and we had been invited to bring a couple of guests and have the works, cocktails, appetizers, extra-thick filet mignons, champagne, anything that was on the menu, in the kitchen or could be procured and that it was all on the house."

"What did he say?"

"He said it sounded good to him. He wanted to know if you were going to be along."

"What did you tell him?"

"I told him, 'Of course!' That you had been the one who had done the job and had the personal contact."

"How did he like that?"

"Well," Bertha said, "he intimated that he'd have preferred just a tête-à-tête with me but his conscience is bothering him just a little. He feels he misjudged you on a couple of cases. He says your only trouble is that you cut corners. . . . Are you going to bring that moon-eyed secretary of yours?"

"I don't think so. She wouldn't enjoy it too much. I'll take her out on my own sometime."

"I'll bet you will," Bertha said.

"There's one other reason I'm not going to take her."

"What reason?"

"The same reason that is going to cause you to ring up Sergeant Sellers and tell him that the invitation is off."

The smile left Bertha's face. Her mouth was hard. Her eyes glittered. "What the hell are you talking about?" she asked. "I thought you said you did the job okay."

"I did."

"Well, that was part of the pay for the job."

"Hasn't Baffin rung up yet?" I asked.

"No."

"Well, he will," I said. "He'll ring up and tell you that the invitation is off; that I'm a so-and-so; that the agency gave him a double cross and he wants his money back."

"How come?"

"I didn't play the game the way he wanted."

Bertha's face darkened. "Damn it, Donald!" she said. "You're too damn independent. This Baffin is a good client. That's the kind of business we want to cultivate. We—"

The phone rang.

Bertha hesitated a moment, snapped the phone up from the cradle and said, "All right, who is it? . . ." There was a moment's silence, then she said, "Oh, yes, Mr. Baffin."

She waited and glared at me.

Gradually her color came back to normal, her mouth

twisted in a smile. "Well, that's very nice, Mr. Baffin," she said. "We'll be there. About eight o'clock? . . . Right . . . How did everything work out last night? All right? . . . No, I haven't had a chance to talk with him about it. He just came in. . . . I see. Well, Sergeant Sellers will be glad to go with us. I told him the truth. I told him we'd done a job for you and that you had invited us to a dinner that was all on the house, steak, champagne, appetizers, the works. . . . Well, that's very fine. . . . Yes, I will, Mr. Baffin . . . yes, he is. . . . Well, he likes to do things his own way, but his own way always produces results. . . . Yes, indeed . . . about eight o'clock then? . . . Oh, a couple of cocktails will be all any of us need. . . . Yes, indeed. Goodbye."

Bertha looked up at me with a puzzled expression. "What the hell gave you the idea that he was sore?"

"When I left last night he called me a son of a bitch."

"What did you do to him?"

"Nothing. I didn't handle the thing exactly the way he wanted."

"Well, he told me that. But he told me that you were brilliant; that you had worked things so that there couldn't be any more blackmail; that the more he thought of it, the more he realized what a magnificent job you had done. He wanted to know if I'd been able to get hold of Sergeant Sellers and— Well, you heard the conversation."

"I heard your end of it," I said.

"He was cordial at his end, *very* cordial."

I said, "I don't like it."

"Why?"

"Last night he was mad all the way through."

"Why?"

"The woman gave me the money to pick up the blackmail documents. I picked them up. Baffin said he was our client and that I was to deliver them to him. I told him, 'Nothing doing.' "

"Where are they?"

"In our safe."

"Well, he did pay the money. Don't you think you could give them to him?"

"The fee was paid by Baffin. We were employed to protect the woman in the case. The woman in the case gave me the ten grand that I turned over for the documents."

"I see," Bertha said.

I said, "There's a fine distinction there."

"But if he and the girl are in love and playing footsies, it should be all right."

"Love," I said, "is transient. Sometimes it's very transient."

Bertha said, "Yes, I guess you did the right thing, come to think of it, and that's the way Baffin feels. He had a night to think it over. He says you did the smart thing."

"I don't like it," I said.

"Don't like what?"

"Baffin saying I did the smart thing."

"You did it, didn't you?"

"I think so."

"Then what don't you like about it?"

"Baffin has had a drastic change of heart and—I don't like the way he's acting."

"Why?"

"I don't know. Call it just a hunch, but it may be that this dinner is more important than we've been led to believe."

"It's for free," Bertha said, "and it's tax free. By God, Donald, do you realize I've been trying to take off weight and it doesn't do a damn bit of good? I'm a hundred and sixty-five pounds no matter how hungry I get, so I've decided to let my hair down and have this one good meal."

I said, "It may be Baffin wants this dinner a lot more than you do. It may mean a great deal to him."

"Well, he was frank with us on that," Bertha said. "He said that people were keeping him under surveillance and if it appeared that he was friendly with Cool and Lam and all palsy-walsy with Sergeant Frank Sellers it would help him a lot."

"Okay," I said. "I've spoken my piece. You still want to go?"

"I'm going," Bertha said. "You're going. Sergeant Sellers is going. And if you want to bring that moon-eyed secretary, I'll try to be nice to her."

"When you try to be nice to another woman," I said, "it's like a cement mixer trying to walk on tiptoe."

"You go to hell!" Bertha flared.

I started for the door.

"Frank Sellers is going to pick me up and take me to Baffin's Grill," she said. "We'll meet you there at eight o'clock."

"You want me to ride with you and Frank?" I asked her.

"I do not!" she snapped.

Chapter 5

Just before lunch the phone rang. Elsie Brand took the call and turned to me, "A Mr. Starman Calvert wants to talk with you. He says that you know him."

She raised her eyebrows questioningly.

I nodded and picked up the instrument in my private office, "Hello," I said.

Starman Calvert's voice crackled over the line, "Hello, sucker!"

"To whom do you think you're talking?" I asked.

"Donald Lam," he said.

"Right," I told him.

"Sucker," he said.

I didn't say anything.

"You thought you were so damn smart last night,"

he said. "I just wanted to tell you how badly you messed up the deal."

"Is this gratuitous," I asked, "or do you want something?"

He said, "Since you have brought it up, I want something and I'm going to get what I want.

"You were so smart last night that you double-crossed your client. You've left yourself wide open, and I'm going to move in.

"You had the whip hand last night, or thought you did, and you were trying all sorts of shenanigans. Today the situation is different and I'm in the saddle. You left a loophole that enabled me to get into the driver's seat. Boy, when your client finds out what I'm going to do next, he's really going to tear his hair. And when he tears his hair, your reputation as the fair-haired boy child is going down the drain."

Calvert's laugh was a harsh rasp of sound.

"Am I supposed to ask questions?" I asked.

"You're supposed to ask questions," he said, "but I'm not going to answer them unless I feel like it."

"Why did you call me?"

"Just to keep you from preening your feathers this morning and thinking how smart you were last night. I haven't told your client yet, but when I do you'll be hearing from him."

"And when am I to expect this will happen?"

"I'm not in a position to make my demands on him right away, but you'll be hearing from him before midnight and when you hear from him he'll be in a panic."

"And there's something that you want?" I asked.

He laughed and said, "That's the good old private detective technique, keep 'em talking. Don't get mad. Don't lose your head. Just hang on and keep 'em talking—and probably you've got a secretary trying to trace this call—I don't even give a damn. I'll tell you where I'm calling from and give you the phone number if you want."

He paused.

I said, "I don't want. I just wanted to hear what you had in mind."

"All right," he said, "I'll tell you this much. I didn't like the idea of having my fingerprints taken."

"I gathered as much."

"When you made me put my fingerprints on that paper you *really* made me sore, and when you made me sore, you opened the door for trouble, lots of trouble."

"My trouble?"

"Your trouble," he said. "Baffin's trouble. Trouble all around."

"And what about the fingerprints, what's so bad about them?"

"I didn't like the idea, that's all. I don't have any criminal record, and you can't tie anything on to me in connection with those fingerprints. But I just didn't like the idea. Now, I'll tell you what, Lam, I want to get back that statement I signed. I'll give you a receipt

for ten thousand dollars, and if you'll meet me half-
way, I'll guarantee that I'm not going to try to put the
bite on anyone else or put another bite on Baffin. But
I want that statement with the fingerprints back, and
I want an assurance from you that you haven't made
any photostatic copies. And I want an apology from
you for your high-handed treatment last night."

"And if you don't get what you want?" I asked.

He said, "You're going to wish you'd been a little
bit less clever and a little bit less arrogant when you
were in a position to call the shots. However, I'm going
to protect you and let you save face. I'm going to have
Baffin instruct you to return that statement to me, together with the fingerprints, provided you co-operate
with me."

"Have you talked with Baffin about that yet?"

"Not yet, but I will."

"When?"

"Sometime tonight," he said, "and when I talk with
Baffin, he'll do exactly what I tell him to do. And before I get done with you, Donald Lam, you'll either
beg my pardon, or you'll be one sorry son of a bitch."

He hung up the phone.

I dropped the instrument back into its cradle and
called to Elsie Brand in the next office. "If Starman
should call up again, tell him that I'm busy and have
no time to talk with him. Did you monitor the conversation?"

She nodded, her eyes wide with apprehension. "Donald, he sounds dangerous!"

"He *tried* to sound dangerous," I said. "A blackmailer's threats are just so much talk as far as we are concerned."

I grinned reassuringly at Elsie and walked out.

Chapter 6

Baffin's Grill was a swank eating place.

A huge electric sign spelled B-A-F-F-I-N-'S for about three seconds; then the letters suddenly changed to G-R-I-L-L.

Four or five young fellows were waiting around in front to park the cars of customers.

I turned the agency heap over to one of the young men in uniform.

He said, "What name?"

I said, "Donald Lam."

"Oh, yes, Mr. Lam. I'm instructed to take care of you. Your car will be parked in a choice spot and ready for you whenever you want to come out."

I offered him a tip. He brushed it aside, "Instructions

from headquarters," he said. "This is on the house."

I went in.

People were lined up in the lobby, waiting for tables. The bar was crowded.

Baffin was standing by the reservations book. He came running out to greet me. "Well, well, Lam! I'm sure glad you could make it! Your partner is already upstairs. We've set up a table on the second floor for your party."

Baffin's Grill had three floors, and elevators.

Baffin personally escorted me to the elevator.

"You'll forgive me being a little hotheaded last night, Lam," he said.

The elevator door opened. He followed me in, punched button No. 2.

The cage moved slowly upwards.

"I was a little excited last night," he explained. "Things were coming pretty fast. After I got to thinking things over, I realized with what consummate skill you had handled the matter. I don't think it's possible for any repercussions, any further bites."

"You sounded plenty peeved last night," I said.

"I was," he admitted, and then added after a moment, "Last night."

The cage stopped. The door opened. Baffin, bowing ceremoniously, ushered me out into a big dining room.

Around the side of the room were curtained booths. In the center were fifteen or twenty tables. The people in the booths had a good deal of privacy. The people in the center tables were on exhibition.

We were going to be on exhibition. Bertha Cool and Frank Sellers stuck out like a sore thumb.

Baffin made a ceremony out of escorting me over to the table and holding a chair for me, then he faded obsequiously into the background and toward the elevator.

Sellers looked up from his cocktail.

Bertha beamed her polite smile.

Sellers said, "Hello, Pint Size."

I grinned. "How are you tonight, Sergeant?"

"Amiable." Sellers grinned. "Amiable and hungry."

Sellers raised his cocktail. "I'm not supposed to be doing this," he went on, "but I have sort of a special dispensation and tonight is my night to howl. Boy, am I hungry! I passed up lunch."

"So did I," Bertha admitted.

I settled myself in the chair. A waiter hovered over me solicitously. "Your dinner is being prepared, sir, but if you'd like a cocktail. . ."

"I'll have a Manhattan," I said.

The waiter was back in a few moments with the cocktail. I raised the glass, nodded over the brim to Bertha and to Sergeant Sellers. "Here's to crime," I said.

They drank with me.

A waiter put a tray of appetizers on the table, caviar, hot cheese tidbits, and potato chips with a dip that had an elusive flavor.

From then on things started moving fast. A waiter brought in a silver cooling bucket with a magnum of champagne.

Sellers settled back with an anticipatory grin and said, "This is the life! What kind of a job did you do for Baffin, Pint Size?"

"Nothing much," I said. "I just handled a pay-off for him."

Sellers' eyes showed interest. "Blackmail?" he asked.

"I don't think so. He was only involved incidentally. Actually I was working for another person, but Baffin was grateful."

"I'll say he was grateful," Sellers said. "Get a lot more clients like this and keep inviting me out."

"Thanks," I told him, "I will."

Then suddenly his eyes were sharp with suspicion. "But keep your nose clean," he warned.

"I try to."

"You're smart," Sellers admitted grudgingly. "Sometimes I think you're too damn smart."

"I haven't hurt *you* any," I told him.

"No," Sellers admitted thoughtfully, after a moment's silence. "You haven't hurt me any; you've done me some good but you've scared me to death. You like to skate on thin ice and you drag me along after you. So far you haven't smashed through and got me in over my head, but there have been times when the ice was creaking like hell."

I let him have the last word. After all, it was a social party. I sipped my drink and didn't say anything.

The dinner moved along at just the right pace. A lobster cocktail with tender chunks of succulent meat, onion soup, a tossed salad, and then the steaks. The champagne flowed like water.

The cooking of those steaks was a masterpiece. The filet mignons must have been two and a half inches thick after they were cooked, and instead of having a well-cooked rim on the outside and raw meat on the inside, they had been charcoal broiled to a uniform red all the way through.

The steak knives were so sharp that they melted right through the meat without bruising the fibers or squeezing out any of the juice. And those steaks were so juicy that, after a couple of cuts, the plate was colored with rich, red steak juice.

Bertha unashamedly sopped her garlic bread in the steak juice and after a moment we followed suit.

There were stuffed baked potatoes and the champagne bubbled in glasses which were kept filled right up to the rim.

Sellers and Bertha began to feel good.

I wasn't doing too bad myself, but I was holding back. There was something about this dinner that bothered me. I didn't like it.

Bertha and Frank were grinning at each other whenever their eyes met. They were two hard-boiled campaigners who were veterans in the game, who didn't give a damn for anybody or anything and wanted the world to know it.

I kept myself to the conversational sidelines.

Our table was right in the center of the room. Everybody could see us and the sort of deluxe dinner we were having—everyone, that is, except the people in the booths.

The booths were occupied mostly by young couples who discreetly moved along the rim of the dining room, following a waiter who kept very much to the shadows until he pulled back a curtain.

The rim of the dining room was a shadow compared with the brightly illuminated center of the room, and we were in the brightest of the illumination.

The restaurant was busy. The dining room was filled. There was a scattering of celebrities, including the columnist, Colin Ellis. A waiter approached our table. "Could you take a phone call, Mr. Lam?" he asked. "The person on the phone says it's a matter of life or death."

I excused myself.

Bertha and the police sergeant hardly noticed my departure.

I followed the waiter to a phone in the lounge.

I picked up the instrument, said, "Hello," and waited. A high-pitched, excited voice said, "It's a frame-up. Don't go for it. Watch your step. It's a trap."

"What is?" I asked.

"Don't be a square. You're being framed."

The party at the other end hung up.

I wasted a little time getting the phone operator of the Grill exchange. I didn't learn anything.

After a bit I threaded my way back.

A trim-figured waitress skirted the shadowy perimeter. She was carrying a tray loaded with food, carrying it as a professional carries it, part of the tray resting on the palm of her right hand, part of it on her right shoulder. She was a neat package.

I was blocking her way.

She looked around helplessly, and I pushed back against the curtain of a booth, not parting the curtains more than an inch or two, just partially entering the booth to give her room to get by.

She gave me a glance of gratitude that was a caress and said, "Thank you, you're very considerate."

I said over my shoulder, in case there were any occupants of the booth, "Pardon me, I'm just clearing a passageway for a waitress."

The waitress passed. I went back to our table. Bertha was talking. Sellers, his face flushed, barely looked up as I seated myself.

Another waitress approached booth thirteen, the one I had backed into. She was carrying a tray with a Chinese dinner, pork spareribs, rice, noodles.

I was watching her as she threw back the curtain of the booth.

She looked inside for a long moment, then she stepped back.

Suddenly she screamed, a shrill piercing scream.

She seemed to wobble for a moment; then her knees gave way and she went to the floor with the dishes on the tray making a crash that attracted as much attention as her scream.

The curtain on the booth fell back into place.

For a moment there was a stunned silence. People sat looking at each other and at the crumpled figure on the floor. Then some man jumped up and ran to the waitress. He bent over her.

The headwaiter suddenly appeared from nowhere, detoured past the waitress and the food on the floor, pulled back the curtain of the booth and looked inside.

Frank Sellers looked at me and said, "What the hell did you do to that waitress back there?"

"I didn't do anything," I told him.

"You were making a pass at her. I saw you."

"You're thinking of another waitress at another place," I said.

The headwaiter burst from the booth and started running. He yelled, "Murder," then got control of himself and slowed to a fast walk.

Abruptly Sellers pushed back his chair and made for the exit.

"What the hell is all this about?" Bertha asked.

The waitress who had spilled the food was on her feet now. She, too, was headed for the serving kitchen. The food and dishes remained on the floor.

The crowd abruptly divided itself into two component parts. Couples who were frankly curious—the ones who were there with their wives; and other couples consisting mostly of older men with younger women. This latter group started melting away, fast.

One or two of the men tossed a bill on the table as they left their unfinished food. Others just made for the door, and to hell with the check. It was too much of a stampede for the waiters to curb the exodus.

I looked at Bertha.

Bertha used her favorite expression. "Fry me for an oyster," she said.

"And then interrogate you as a witness?" I asked her.

Bertha's face flushed. "What's the meaning of that crack?" she asked, her diamond-hard eyes glittering with the moisture that comes from alcoholic consumption.

"Why do you think Frank Sellers made it a point to get out of here so fast?" I asked.

Bertha cocked her eyebrows in silent inquiry.

"Think of the headlines," I said. "MURDER COMMITTED WITHIN FIFTY FEET OF POLICE SERGEANT."

"That's an angle, all right," Bertha said.

"Then," I told her, "Frank Sellers gets on the witness stand. Lawyers fire questions at him. Which way was he facing? What did he see? Why didn't he see more? Who entered the booth? Who came out? Then, comes the pay-off question. 'How much had you been drinking, Sergeant?'

"If he saw anything at all, the defense attorney riddles him with cross-examination. If he didn't see anything, the D.A. wants to know if he wouldn't have seen something if he hadn't been drunk."

Bertha's chair scraped as she pushed it back.

"Let's get the hell out of here, Donald," she said.

"We're on our way," I told her.

All the people who had left the restaurant in a panic were jammed in a tight knot on the sidewalk in front of the entrance to the Grill. Some of them were waving bills at the car hops, asking for fast service.

I caught the eye of my car hop.

He said, "Just a minute, Mr. Lam."

I shook my head and said, "*Now,*" and handed him a five-dollar bill.

He gave one look at the bill, grinned, and said, "*Now!*"

He had the car up in front within a matter of seconds. I started to help Bertha in.

"To hell with that polite stuff, get around behind the wheel and get me out of here!" Bertha snapped.

We got out. I drove her home. She was silently thoughtful.

"It might be a good idea if we were both called out of town on business," I said.

"Have we done anything to be ashamed of?" she asked.

"Not yet," I said and drove off.

Chapter 7

I never did find out how Frank Sellers got the unlisted number of my apartment—probably through Bertha —but the phone was ringing as I fitted the latchkey to the door and entered.

I picked up the phone. "Hello."

"Lam?"

"That's right, Frank."

"That dinner tonight," he said, "you were called away. A waiter came with a message and asked you to take a phone call."

"Right."

"I want to tell you about that phone call," he said.

"What about it?"

"That," he said, "was a phone call from my partner,

Gillis Adams, telling you to tell me that he had an important clue in a case we're investigating and he wanted to talk with me right away."

"Why did he call me instead of you?"

"He was afraid they'd have to page the name and he didn't want my name to go out over the loudspeaker, so he decided to call you and relay the message through you."

"That's a good story," I said, "any proof of it?"

"You."

"Any other corroboration?"

"My partner remembers the incident very clearly."

"Where are you now?"

"In a Turkish bath, you damn fool," Sergeant Sellers said, "and when I get rid of this alcoholic halitosis and sweat that goddam champagne out of me, I'll go to headquarters all starry-eyed and innocent.

"And then tomorrow I'm going to tear that Baffin's Grill apart. This thing stinks."

"In what way?"

"It was a frame-up, a setup. If I'd gone over to that booth and even so much as looked inside, I'd have been busted. You know it, and I know it."

"Know who the corpse was?" I asked.

"Not officially."

"Unofficially?"

"Unofficially, I am given to understand the guy was named Starman Calvert. The papers in his wallet show that he was married and lived in the Dromedary

Apartments. When police went there to notify his wife, there was no one home and Mrs. Calvert still hasn't returned."

"What was Calvert's occupation?" I asked.

"That," Frank Sellers said, "is something I was going to ask you about."

"Why me?"

"I was just wondering if perhaps you might have known the guy."

"What's the description?" I asked.

"Age forty-two, weight a hundred and sixty-five, height five feet ten inches, dark wavy hair, blue eyes, gray mustache."

"I think I've met him somewhere," I said, "but for the life of me I can't tell you just where."

"Let's not kid ourselves, that dinner was a frame-up. If you had any part in it, I'm going to work you over with a rubber hose, load you in a taxicab, and send you home. You'll be in bed for a couple of days at least."

"If it was a frame-up, we were *all* framed," I said.

"I'm not so sure," Sellers said. "It's the capital M, capital O that I'm thinking of."

"Modus Operandi?" I asked.

"That's right," he said, "Modus Operandi. That's the way we solve about ninety per cent of our cases. These damn daring schemes remind me of your type of Modus Operandi. If you're mixed up in this, I'll pin that murder on you if it's the last thing I do. There were witnesses who *saw* you coming out of that booth."

"Not coming out," I said. "I backed in against the curtains in order to let a waitress go by."

"Coming out," Sellers said. "Two witnesses so far. I saw you myself just as you left the booth. Right now we can play it either way we want. You can be a witness or a suspect."

"No one saw me leaving that booth," I said. "I wasn't in it."

"*I* saw you coming out myself," Sellers said.

"Did you, indeed, Sergeant?" I asked, "and what were *you* doing there, by the way?"

"I think," he said, "I was being setup as a Patsy, and when I find out all the facts I'm going to give somebody a damn good working over—do you get that, Pint Size, a damn good working over!"

And Sellers hung up.

I always keep a suitcase and a bag ready packed for a quick airplane trip in case of necessity. Now I took the suitcase and bag down to the agency car and got out of there fast. I went to the Restabit Motel. I could claim that I was working on the case there, and I didn't dare register under an assumed name. That could be taken as evidence of flight. I wasn't at all certain that eventually I wouldn't be standing trial for the murder of Starman Calvert.

Chapter 8

I slept like a log until eight o'clock. Then the noise of construction on the apartment house across the street filled the neighborhood.

The murder in the Grill would have been too late for details in the morning papers, but I turned on the radio and the eight-thirty broadcast had it in detail. "Cop misses murder case by a matter of inches," the announcer said, by way of headlines.

Then he went on, "Only the fact that Sergeant Sellers of the Homicide Squad was called away from his dinner at a well-known downtown grill by an emergency prevented him from being a witness in a murder case which has so far proven particularly baffling to the police.

"Starman Calvert, of the Dromedary Apartments, was found dead in a booth in the famous Baffin's Grill. He had been stabbed in the back with a long-bladed butcher knife, and death had been almost instantaneous, according to the police surgeon who examined the body.

"Not only was the second floor of the Grill, where the murder took place, crowded at the time, but Sergeant Frank Sellers of the Homicide Squad had been dining there with friends. A few moments before the murder he had been summoned to headquarters by a telephone message regarding an emergency development in a case which Sergeant Sellers and his partner, Gillis Adams, were working on.

"It wasn't until after Sergeant Sellers arrived at headquarters that he learned that a murder had been committed at the Grill where he had been having dinner, and the murder must have been committed within a matter of minutes, perhaps seconds, after he had left the place.

" 'To think,' Gillis Adams said, 'that if I hadn't put through that emergency call, asking Frank Sellers to get in touch with me right away, Frank might have been on the scene at the time of the murder. And because Sergeant Sellers is a trained observer, he would have noticed anyone leaving booth thirteen where the murder was committed. In fact, he might even have apprehended the murderer in the act of making his escape.' "

The announcer went on to state, "Starman Calvert was living at the Dromedary Apartments, but neighbors knew very little about him. His wife, an attractive blonde, is reported to be a buyer for a large, downtown department store and is at present away on a buying trip. Police are trying to locate her as she has not as yet been notified of her husband's tragic death."

Then the announcer went on to talk about the weather and the stock market.

I sat there in front of the radio without hearing the words that were being said, thinking of my position.

Gillis Adams was covering for Sellers. I was also supposed to cover for Sellers. If I didn't back the officers up, my name was mud. If I did back them up, I would be juggling the time element in a murder case and there was always the possibility that the time element might turn out to be important.

It was indeed a remarkable coincidence that Baffin had arranged for a dinner party at which Frank Sellers would be present at the very moment the blackmailer was being murdered.

In that event Baffin must have known in advance almost the exact time the murder was going to be committed. And when a man knows in advance when a murder is going to be committed, he's either a murderer, a clairvoyant, a conspirator or a very material witness.

Under those circumstances, my best bet was to keep

myself out of circulation so I couldn't be called on to commit myself one way or another.

If Sellers asked me to back up an alibi and I turned him down, I'd have burned my bridges. If I backed him up, I'd have painted myself into a corner.

I shut off the radio, walked to the window, and looked out across the parking lot to where the apartment house was going up.

Men were swarming around on the framework like ants. Big cranes were lifting steel girders into place. It was an ant heap of activity.

I had breakfast in the motel dining room, stopped at the desk, said I would probably stay over for another day and paid in advance. Then I went outside and took some pictures.

An eleven o'clock news broadcast on television had a little more information about the murder. Police were still unable to locate Mrs. Calvert. Despite the fact she was said to be a buyer or an assistant buyer for a large downtown department store, none of the big stores had been able to furnish any information.

According to neighbors who had talked with her in the apartment house, she traveled extensively on business trips, flying to Chicago and New York several times a month, making an occasional trip to Paris. She was reported to be very cultured, very sophisticated and she held herself pretty much aloof.

Police had asked for help in trying to locate her so as to inform her of her husband's tragic demise.

The crime itself was baffling.

The waitress who had discovered the body told police that Calvert had ordered a double Chinese dinner, stating that he expected a companion to join him by the time the dinner was ready to be served, but he was alone when he entered the booth and was alone when his body was found.

When the waitress had entered the booth with the food, she had found Calvert's body slumped forward on the table, his head in his hands, the handle of the big knife protruding from his back.

Police had as yet been unable to trace the weapon. It was a sharp, long-bladed butcher knife which had seen quite a bit of professional use. Police felt that the razor-sharp edge, the well-worn handle, all indicated the knife was one which had been used either in a restaurant kitchen or in a butcher shop.

One witness had seen a man in his late twenties or early thirties, slight of build, apparently emerging from booth thirteen just as a waitress had passed with a tray loaded with food. The waitress and this man had, according to the witness, exchanged a few brief words about some matter which they had in common. The witness felt certain from the facial expressions that the couple were not strangers. There was, as he expressed it, "an air of intimacy" between the two.

The witness felt he would be able to identify the man if he saw him again.

I switched off the television.

That's the worst of the eyewitness. He sees something in a fragmentary manner. He remembers only a part of what he has seen. His memory is inaccurate, his vision is inaccurate, and nine times out of ten his imagination supplies details his eyes never saw.

I had backed into the booth when the waitress walked by. I hadn't even really parted the curtains, but when I stepped back after the waitress had gone by, someone happened to have seen me and had taken it for granted that I was emerging from the booth. He saw the brief verbal exchange with the waitress.

Then the witness had gone back to his chitchat and hadn't even noticed that I had walked over to another table and sat down. That witness would be duck soup for Frank Sellers if I didn't co-operate. It would take only a little bit of elementary suggestion to have this witness believing that he had seen me emerging from booth thirteen just before the murder was discovered.

I looked up the home address of Nicholas Baffin and called him on the phone.

"Baffin?" I asked when he answered.

"Who is this?" he asked suspiciously.

"Donald Lam."

"Oh, yes."

"Police out there?"

"Not now."

"They have been?"

"Yes."

"I'm coming out," I said.

"Don't do that," he told me. "Good heavens, not out here!"

"I think that's the best place for me to see you," I said.

"No, no, not here."

"The Grill?"

"No, not there, either. Where are you calling from?"

"A phone booth," I said.

"What do you want to see me about?"

"I just want to talk with you," I said. "You wait right there, I'm coming out!"

"No, no, you mustn't come out here."

"I'm coming" I said, and hung up the phone.

From the telephone booth, I rang the office and asked for Elsie Brand. When I had her on the line, I said, "Elsie, I'm doing field work on an important blackmail case. I'll try and keep in touch with you, but I won't be in the office and you can't reach me. Just take any messages that come in and sit tight."

"Okay," she said. "Bertha is very anxious to talk with you. She told me that if you called she had to talk with you."

"Put her on," I told Elsie.

"Just a minute, I'll get through on the switchboard."

After a moment, I heard Bertha's voice all honey and cream. "Hello, Donald," she said, "and how are *you* this morning?"

"Fine."

"Are you coming in soon?"

"No."

"When?"

"I don't know, I'm doing legwork on an important case."

"Donald, I want to talk with you to be sure that we understand each other."

"In what way?"

"About what happened last night."

"What happened?"

"Well, of course, it was that unfortunate incident. We were dining, and you and I had had some champagne, but Frank Sellers wasn't drinking because he was on duty.

"Then you got this call from Gillis Adams, telling you to get Frank Sellers up to headquarters right away on an important matter, and Frank left about a minute before the waitress entered the booth and screamed."

She stopped, waiting for me to say something. I wadded my handkerchief into the mouthpiece of the telephone and said, "I can hardly hear you, Bertha, what are you talking about?"

I heard Bertha say, "Damn it to hell, this telephone service is terrible. *I* can't hear *you*—just barely hear a word."

"What did you say?"

"I said I could barely hear you. You sound like you're a million miles away."

"Who's a million miles away?"

"You are!"

"Where?" I asked.

"Oh, damn it," Bertha said, "call me back on another line. Let's get a better connection. I'm talking important business."

"What's the business connection?" I yelled.

"Call again," Bertha screamed.

She slammed up the phone at her end.

I took my wadded handkerchief out of the mouthpiece, hung up the telephone and went out to see Nicholas Baffin.

The Baffin house was an anachronism. It had been built a generation ago when domestic help was readily available. It was an aristocratic mansion in a row of aristocratic mansions.

They were hanging on the edge of an economic precipice now. The land was getting more valuable, the buildings were tax liabilities, becoming larger white elephants with the passing of each day. A block down the street one of the buildings had been converted into a secretarial school; another one into a medical clinic, but the Baffin place was standing in stately majesty with its curved driveway, its palm trees and its aura of futile respectability.

Baffin was coldly furious. "You have no right to come here, Lam," he said.

"I had to talk with you."

"I am at my office every afternoon at three o'clock."

"What I'm talking about won't wait until three

o'clock. What the hell was the idea of having us decoy Frank Sellers into your place just when a murder was being committed?"

"Do you, for one minute, think that I had any knowledge a murder was going to be committed?"

"Then it was a remarkable coincidence."

"Lam," he said, "I don't care to talk with you. You may not know it, but you're hotter than a stove lid."

"How come?"

"Two people saw you coming out of booth thirteen within less than two minutes of the time the murder was discovered. You've been positively identified.

"The police aren't saying anything as yet, but they're holding the matter open for further inquiry."

"Did you," I asked, "know this man Calvert was going to be at the Grill?"

"Of course not. Don't be silly! I had you handle the pay-off because I never wanted to see him again. That was your job."

"Did you see him at the Grill?"

"Of course not."

"Did you kill him?"

Baffin's eyes narrowed. "Look, Lam, this is a dog-eat-dog world. If you even intimate I might have murdered the guy, I'll have you convicted before you can catch your breath. I'm no pantywaist to be pushed around. I have connections. I can be tough."

"Keep talking," I said. "You interest me."

He said, "Later on today the police are going to

question me about you, about the occasion for you and your partner being in the dining room as my guests. I'm going to tell them."

"About the blackmail?" I asked.

"I'm going to tell them that I had hired you to do a job, and that you double-crossed me."

"And for that reason you gave me a complimentary dinner?" I asked.

I saw the doubt flash across his eyes as he realized the position in which he had put himself.

"Now then," I went on, "*I'm* going to tell *you* something. I don't know what kind of a game you're playing, but you've overlooked one thing that you'd better know about before you get your feet wet."

"My feet are not going to get wet," he said.

I said, "That picture that was taken of you and Connie getting in the car at the motel—"

"Shut up, you damn fool," he interrupted, lowering his voice to almost a whisper. "My wife is in the house!"

I said, "I just wanted to tell you that picture wasn't a stolen picture taken by a blackmailer. It was a posed picture."

"What!" he exclaimed.

I said, "Your attitude is frozen. A fill-in flash was used so your hat brim wouldn't shade your features, and your face was turned so that the light caught it just right. You knew the picture was being taken. You even had the car parked so the sunlight shone on the license plate, and I think the license plate had been cleaned up so that the number would be perfectly legible. The picture wasn't taken with available light. It was a flash-fill."

He sat there, just looking at me.

After a while, he said, "When did you get this idea?"

"As soon as I saw the picture," I told him. "I've done enough candid photography to know a posed picture when I see one. In my business we have to use cameras to take surreptitious pictures, and when you use a camera under available light conditions you always have certain technical defects. When you take people in motion, there's a certain dynamic symmetry about the picture, and usually a little blur. That picture you got from Calvert was as phony as a three-dollar bill. It had been posed. You had very carefully put down the suitcase, had put your arm on Connie's elbow, had turned your face so the light was on it at just the right angle, had said something to Connie so she was looking at you and then waited to be sure the picture was snapped at the appropriate moment.

"If you want to know, that's one of the big reasons I didn't give you the picture. Since Connie was our client and since there was no reason to believe Connie had been in on the frame-up with the photographer, I decided your interests were adverse to hers.

"At the time I felt that you were in cahoots with the blackmailer and that the whole thing was a scheme to shake Connie Alford down for ten grand. I didn't think you needed the money that bad, but I couldn't be sure. I was just riding along to get the sketch."

I stopped talking, and Baffin said, "You son of a bitch!" but this time there was no anger, only awed admiration in his voice.

I sat there without saying anything.

At length he said, "I goofed."

"You goofed," I agreed.

"You, however, were mistaken in assuming that I was connected with the blackmailer, at least to the extent of sharing in the money."

"Talk some more," I told him.

He said, "This was being done to *protect* Connie."

"Some protection!" I said sarcastically.

"No, no, you don't understand. She was in San Francisco on the morning of the sixth. It was necessary to have proof that she was in Los Angeles and had been in Los Angeles over the weekend. This blackmail setup looked like a perfect way to do the job. Particularly, when I got a private detective to make the pay-off."

I didn't say anything. He sat there.

"Want to tell me more about it?" I asked.

"No," he said.

There was more silence.

After a while, he went on, "If you'd give me those pictures and let me destroy them, and then you could testify afterwards that the pictures showed Connie Alford and me in front of the car in the parking space at the motel, and testify that the registration card showed on the evening of the fifth . . ." His voice trailed away into hopeful silence.

I didn't say anything.

He went on, "There might be another ten grand in it for you, personally."

I said, "I don't think you appreciate my position. As far as I'm concerned, I'm working for Connie Alford. Whatever is for her best interests registers with me, but I'm not suborning perjury for anyone."

He sat for a good minute thinking things over; then abruptly got to his feet, "Lam," he said, "don't say anything about this to anybody. I think you'd better go now. I'll be in touch with you later on." And then he added, ruefully, "This is one hell of a development."

He escorted me to the door.

As he opened the door of his study, a woman came from the spacious parlor and started moving through the hallway. She began to ascend the staircase, stopped when she saw us, and regarded me with frank curiosity.

She was considerably younger than Nick Baffin, a blonde who was a perfectionist. She had given careful attention to her hair, her eyebrows, her make-up, her dress, even her manner of walking. Everything she did was rehearsed, planned, carefully plotted.

"Oh, good morning, dear," Baffin said.

"Hello, *darling*."

She stood still, looking at me, apparently awaiting an introduction.

"I'll be right with you, dear," Baffin said, and all but pushed me out the door.

A car was parked next to mine. It was a big Cad, and I checked the license number, just in case. It was HGS 609. Evidently his wife had just driven up in it, and I would have bet fifty dollars against a plugged nickel she had already checked the registration card in the agency automobile I was driving and had jotted down the license number for future reference. She was that sort of woman.

Baffin gave one helpless look at the Cadillac and I could read the thought that was running through his mind.

"You shouldn't have come out here, Lam," he said as he escorted me out the front door.

"You shouldn't have held out on me, Baffin," I said as I walked down the steps.

He stood watching me until I had slammed the door of the agency car, started the motor and had the wheels rolling down the driveway.

I stopped at the first phone booth I came to and called Elsie Brand.

"A woman by the name of Connie Alford will be calling," I said. "Tell her to leave her address and phone number."

"Okay," she said. "Sergeant Sellers wants you to call as soon as you come in."

"I haven't been in, have I?"

"No."

"Then I can't call," I told her. "Be a good girl."

I hung up before she could give me any more messages.

Chapter 9

I listened to the radio news broadcast and also tuned in on the television resumé of what was happening in the city.

Police were very much concerned at their inability to get a line on Mrs. Starman Calvert. It was definitely determined that she was not employed by any local department store.

A Mrs. Starman Calvert had been located in San Francisco. She said she had divorced her husband five years before and had no knowledge that he had remarried. She was a brunette, forty-five and fat.

I filled the agency car with gas and started cruising in the vicinity of the Dromedary Apartments. I made a survey of the filling stations. There were only two within ten blocks.

On the first one I drew a blank.

On the second one I went through the routine of showing my credentials and stating that I was representing a client by the name of Calvert whose credit card had been lost. I was trying to find if someone had picked it up and had been using it, I said. There were indications that the pickpocket who took it resided in the neighborhood and what I was trying to get was proof that would support a conviction.

I talked fast. The attendant didn't think fast.

He said I was welcome to look at the records he had which hadn't been turned in. He went to the office and after a few moments called me in to look at a stack of cards. One of them had the signature of Mrs. Starman Calvert.

I pretended to be comparing the signature with a card I took from my pocket.

"No, this isn't the one," I said, and looked for the license on the automobile.

"I will, however, make a note of the number of the card," I said, "just in case."

I whipped out my notebook and wrote down the license number of the automobile which had been serviced.

The license number was HGS 609 and the make of the car was a Cadillac.

I thanked the guy, put my notebook in my pocket and left.

I went to a phone booth and rang Elsie.

"Could you sneak out for a coffee break?" I asked.

"Sure," she said.

"In the safe," I told her, "in my personal compartment is a brown Manila envelope that has some photographs and some negatives.

"One of the photographs shows a car in front of a motel. The sign on the motel shows in the picture. It's the Restabit. A man and a woman are standing beside the car. A piece of baggage is on the ground, the trunk is open; he's assisting the woman into the car."

"Okay, what do you want?" she asked. "Do you want me to bring the pictures to you?"

"No," I said. "Take that envelope, hold it so that no one can see you're carrying an envelope when you leave the office. Go to the bank downstairs. Ask for the cashier. Tell him you want to rent a safety deposit box in your own name; put the key in your purse and say nothing to anybody.

"Got it?"

"I've got it."

"Okay, good girl," I told her.

"Just a minute, Donald, there's something else," she said. "A call came in, Connie Alford. She wants you to call her. She left a telephone number."

"What's the number?" I asked.

"Six eight four, two three oh eight," she said. "She said it was very important that you get in touch with her at the earliest possible moment."

"Okay, Elsie," I said, "get those papers out of the

office and keep the key in your purse. Don't let *anyone* know what you've done."

"Donald," she asked, "are you getting in trouble over something?"

"I don't know," I told her, "but right now I'm playing 'em pretty close to my chest. You back me up, will you?"

"All the way," she promised.

"Good girl," I said.

I hung up, and then after a moment called the number Elsie had given me for Connie Alford.

A seductive feminine voice answered the telephone.

"Connie?" I asked.

"Oh, yes! Is this Donald?"

"Right."

"Donald, I want to see you. In fact, I *have* to see you. Can I come to your office?"

"No."

"But Donald, it's important!"

I said, "I'd better come to your place."

"Oh, no, this is no place for a visitor."

"Why not?"

"It's just a . . . just a dump."

"You're living there?"

"Yes."

"Where it it?"

"It's called the Danchly Apartments. It's on Milton Street. I'm in three oh five, but Donald, it's just a rooming house, that's all. I'm living in a little cubby-hole."

"What number?"

"Three oh five."

"I'll be there," I told her. "Don't tell anyone I'm coming. Don't tell anyone you've talked to me."

"Isn't there someplace I could meet you? Isn't there—?"

"Not at the moment," I told her. "I'll be there in fifteen or twenty minutes."

"I'll be waiting," she said.

"Baffin told you to call me?" I asked.

She hesitated for three or four seconds, then said, "Yes."

"Are you to report to him that you've made a contact?"

"Not until after I've talked with you."

"Okay," I said, "I'll be out."

I drove conservatively with the agency car, found the Danchly Apartments, got a parking place, and went through the shabby-looking lobby.

The inside of the place smelled of cooking and human occupancy. The corridors were poorly lit. It was a walk-up. Room 305 was on the third floor and back.

I tapped on the door.

Connie Alford, dressed like a million dollars, opened the door and disclosed a room not much bigger than a good-sized closet. There was a single bed, one chair, a dresser and a worn carpet on the floor.

"Oh, Donald," she said, "I hate for you to see me like this!"

"You live here?"

"Yes."

"What about the swank apartment where I saw you night before last?"

"That was all part of the plant."

"What plant?"

She said, "I can't tell you everything, Donald, only that I was masquerading as a successful actress, which I'm not."

She sat on the bed and indicated I was to sit in the straight-backed wobbly chair.

"You have no phone here?"

"Heavens, no. I don't even have a bathroom. The bath is down the hall."

"But you gave me a number to call."

"That's the public telephone."

"And you were waiting there?"

"I was waiting where I could hear the phone, hoping you'd call. Those were my instructions, to wait right by the phone until you called."

"And who gave you those instructions?"

"You know."

"I'm asking who gave you those instructions?"

"Mr. Baffin."

"Did you," I asked, "spend the night in the Restabit Motel with Baffin, any night?"

"No."

"What did you do?"

"We drove up to the motel and parked the car. The photographer was in a car behind us. I was instructed what to do, what position to take, and to look toward the camera. Mr. Baffin directed the whole thing."

"Then he gave you ten thousand dollars to buy the pictures?"

"Yes."

I said, "I suppose you're taking orders from Baffin, but as far as the agency is concerned, we're representing you, not Baffin."

"Why me?"

"Because you gave us the ten grand to protect your good name."

"What good name?" she asked.

"Don't you have one?" I asked.

She shook her head. "No longer."

"You'd better tell me about you," I said.

"Why?"

I said, "A girl with your looks who doesn't have a good name has no business living in a cheap apartment like this."

"Oh, I didn't mean that. I'm not selling anything."

"What are you doing?"

"I wish I knew. I'm just knocking my brains out."

"How come?"

She said, "I guess it's the same old story. I was small-town. A local luncheon club gave a popularity contest.

It was all put over by some outside promoter who came in and made a cleanup.

"The merchants bought votes from the promoter and then distributed those votes with merchandise orders so that people who bought merchandise could vote for the prettiest and most popular girl in town. There were half a dozen candidates and, of course, all of their friends started boosting for them. It made a big deal for the merchants and, of course, a big deal for the promoter."

"You won the contest?"

"Yes."

"What did you win?"

"An all-expense trip to Hollywood, a screen test, a lot of notoriety, and that's all."

"What about the screen test?"

"It was a contract job. It wasn't any studio. It was some photographer who made a screen test."

"What about the contracts?"

"I've looked them over carefully. Actually, there's nothing in them. It says I am to be given a trip to Hollywood and a screen test in Hollywood."

"Return transportation?" I asked.

She laughed bitterly and said, "What girl thinks about return transportation when she's going to Hollywood for a screen test after she's won a beauty contest? I was on cloud nine. I would have done anything just to have had the trip to Hollywood and the screen test. I didn't think about the future."

"Anything about living expenses once you got to Hollywood?"

"Not a word, just the trip to Hollywood and the screen test. That was it."

"How did you meet Baffin?"

"I struck him for a job as a waitress."

"Did you get it?"

"No, he looked me over, asked a lot of questions and told me he thought he could use me in another way. He asked if I'd like two hundred and fifty dollars.

"Asking me if I'd like two hundred and fifty dollars was like asking a starving man if he'd like a good steak dinner."

"So you took him up?"

She nodded.

"What did he want?"

"He wanted me to have a picture taken with him at a motel and swear that I had spent the night of the fifth in the motel with him."

"The picture was actually taken one week later, on the morning of the thirteenth, wasn't it?"

"Yes. How did you know?"

"By the apartment house going up across from the motel. On a deal of that sort the progress of the steel construction is just like dating a picture. The photograph I got from Calvert shows the state of construction on the thirteenth, not on the sixth."

"Have you told Baffin?"

"Not yet. I've told him the picture was posed, with

a fill-in flash. That jolted him. I'm saving the part about the date the picture was taken as a second jolt."

"Don't tell him I let you know about the date."

"I'll have to use my judgment, and you'll have to come clean with me. Remember I'm trying to protect you. Now then, did you know any of the people involved, Starman Calvert, who was supposed to be the blackmailer?"

She shook her head. "All I know is that I was given instructions. Then I was told to check in at the Monarch Grand Apartments where an apartment had been re served for me on a twenty-four hour basis. I was to meet you there and, at the proper time, was to give you ten thousand dollars in cash; then I was to check out.

"I was told to act the part of a very successful star who had the world at her feet and I had some expense money for a hairdresser, a manicure and a real perfumed bath—and how I enjoyed that bath in a real porcelain full-length tub with all the hot water I wanted."

I thought things over.

"Mr. Baffin tells me that I am to tell you that he is my boss and that you're to do what he says."

"We don't take on jobs in that way," I said. "I was told that it was your money that was being put up and that it was your good name we were trying to protect."

She sat there looking at me. "That makes sort of an impasse?" she asked.

I said, "Has Baffin given you any more money?"

"No, just the two hundred and fifty dollars."

"Where are your things?" I asked.

She indicated the space under the bed. "Two suitcases," she said, "and that's it. Naturally, I wanted to buy my new clothes in Hollywood."

"You're looking pretty good now," I said.

"These clothes," she said, "came with the job. That's one thing I didn't mention. He gave me a credit slip to go and buy clothes at a real first-class store. It included the outfit, shoes, stockings, underwear, dress—everything."

"The suitcases are under the bed?" I asked.

She nodded.

I got out of the chair, down on my knees and started hauling out the suitcases.

"What's the matter?" she asked. "Don't you trust me? Do you want to look in them?"

"No," I said, "you're moving out of this dump."

"But Donald, I can't. I'm just as flat broke as—"

"This time I'm picking up the tab," I said.

"What do I have to do?" she asked cautiously.

"Move out," I told her.

"Where?"

"I'll find a place."

"And then what?"

"Then you live there."

"Strings?" she asked.

"No strings."

I went down the hall to the telephone and called Mayme Owens.

We had done a job for her a couple of years ago, and she had been very, very grateful. We always heard from her every Christmas.

I recognized her voice on the phone, but I wanted to make sure. "Mrs. Owens?"

"Yes."

"Donald Lam, Mayme."

"Oh, hello, Donald. How are you? What's new?"

"Lots of things," I said, "but right now, I'm talking business."

"What kind of business?"

"Confidential business."

"What do you want?"

"An apartment."

"What kind of an apartment?"

"A single, pretty good apartment, kitchenette, bath, completely furnished, maid service twice a week."

"For you?"

"A friend."

"Man—woman?"

"Woman."

"References?"

"None necessary."

"Everything all quiet?"

"Quiet and respectable."

She laughed and said, "I have it."

"The name," I told her, "is Connie Alford and we'll

be around within the next thirty minutes to move in."

"We?"

"We," I said.

"If you're moving in with her, Donald, you've got to—"

"No, no," I said, "I'm just furnishing the transportation."

"Wait a minute, Donald, is she hot?"

"Just a little warm, but nothing official."

"You wouldn't get me in trouble?"

"It's been our job to keep you out of trouble," I said.

"I know, and don't think I'm not grateful. Come on around."

"What will the rent be?"

"About as low as any similar place in the city."

"Suits me," I said. "Charge it to me. We're coming right out."

I hung up the phone, walked back to Connie Alford's room and said, "Get the things you're going to need for the next few days packed up. We're on our way."

She stooped down and pulled an opened suitcase from under the bed. It was already half packed with clothes.

"Give me a hand," she said, "and put it back on the bed. When I heard steps in the corridor and heard them stop in front of the door I wasn't certain it was you. So I pushed this back under the bed."

"Good girl," I told her.

She threw some more dresses in the suitcase then

dove under the bed and picked up a handbag. "Close the suitcase and keep your back turned, Donald," she said, "the rest of the stuff is intimate."

She pulled out a drawer and started putting things in the bag behind my back.

Four minutes after I had returned from the telephone she was all finished.

"Did you leave that drawer empty?" I asked.

"Yes. Why?"

"Distribute things around. Put something in it," I said. "An empty drawer looks as though you had dusted out, but leave some clothes and be sure there's something in every drawer."

She started distributing things.

"That okay?" she asked.

"Okay," I said. "Let's go."

She locked the door behind us; we went down the stairs, climbed in the agency car and I took her to meet Mayme Owens.

When Connie saw the new apartment, her eyes bugged.

"Donald," she said, "this is class—first class."

"Mayme Owens runs a nice place," I told her. "She'll be your friend."

"Nice—this is luxury. This is—I can't afford to get used to this, not on my income."

"You won't get used to it within the next two or three days," I told her.

"Don't fool yourself. I can get accustomed to this very, very rapidly."

"Perhaps your income will pick up," I told her.

"I have been hoping that for weeks—Donald, there's no use in my fooling you, I can't begin to pay for this. In fact, I can't pay for any two places to live. I'm not sure I can even keep up the rent on that shabby room that I have."

"That room you have," I told her, "is your business. This apartment is my business. Don't bother about the rent. We'll take care of it."

"What's behind all this?" she asked.

"I don't know," I told her. "I've got to find out. Do you know?"

"No," she admitted.

"All right, stay here and stay under cover. . . . You have yourself listed with various casting agencies?"

"Yes."

"Telephone them every day and see if they have anything for you, and if they have anything, tell them your agent will check on it. Don't give anyone your present address."

She laughed. "I don't have an agent."

"You do now," I said.

"Oh," she said shortly.

I said, "There's a phone here in the apartment. It comes through a central switchboard. There's no service after eleven o'clock at night; no service before six-thirty in the morning, but all other times if you want anything, just pick up that telephone and give the number. There's a long cord on the phone, you can even telephone from bed. Don't let Baffin know where you are. Let him worry."

I opened my wallet and gave her fifty dollars. "Go down to the market and get the pantry stocked up with stuff that you'll need for a day or two," I told her. "Don't go back to the other apartment. Don't go anywhere near it. Don't communicate with anybody except the casting agencies, and don't tell *anyone* where you are.

"Here's the number of the agency. Call—"

"Oh, I have your number. I called and talked with your secretary."

"Who told you to?"

"Nick Baffin."

"Then you were to report to him?"

"I did report. I told him that you were out but that I'd left word."

"Baffin," I said, "will realize that I've taken you out of circulation and put you under cover. He'll start trying to reach you. He'll probably get in touch with the casting agency. It will sound like a job. Be sure to tell the agency that your agent will investigate."

"That's not the way it's done," she said, "not with bit players. You have to be selected and have an audition and—"

"That's the way it's going to be done in your case from now on," I said. "If the offer is bonafide, we'll find some way of making things work. But if it's just a scheme on the part of Baffin to be sure you don't get out from under his thumb, we'll give him the run around."

I started for the door.

"That's all you want, Donald?" she asked.

"That's all."

She came to stand close to me at the door, searching my eyes with hers. At length she said, "Donald, you're a swell guy. I wish I had known there were people like you in the world a few years ago."

Suddenly she was blinking back tears.

Chapter 10

I called the office, got Elsie Brand on the phone and said, "Elsie, you know who this is. Anything doing?"

"Good heavens, is there anything doing!" she exclaimed. "Everybody in the world is looking for you."

"Such as?" I asked.

"Colin Ellis, the newspaper reporter, for one," she said. "Bertha is having kittens because she tried to talk with you but there was a poor phone connection. She's talking about suing the phone company. Frank Sellers wants you to report to him immediately at headquarters, and the girl who says you know only as Lois says it is very important that she talk to you at once."

"Lois?" I asked.

"Her name is Lois Malone, but she says you know

her only as Lois; that that was the name that was
stitched on her blouse."

"She works at Baffin's Grill?" I asked, playing a
hunch.

"She didn't say where she worked. She just said that
it was important that you get in touch with her. She
said that she lives at the Hillcrest Arms Apartments.
She says not to confuse it with the Hillcrest Apartments. Where she lives is the Hillcrest *Arms* Apartments. She left a number that you can call. She has her
own phone."

"Give," I said.

Elsie gave me the number and I wrote it down; then
checked back to make sure I had it right.

"What about her?" Elsie asked.

"Darned if I know, Elsie, but she could be rather
important. I'll give her a jingle. In the meantime, you
haven't heard anything from me."

"Is there any place I can reach you?" she asked.

"Not right now," I said, "but if I don't get things
straightened out within the next twenty-four hours,
you can reach me in jail."

"Oh, you've gone and got into trouble again!"

"I think this time," I said, "trouble has got into me.
Keep cool, Elsie. Don't panic, and don't give anybody
any information."

I hung up and called the number Elsie had given me.

A young, well-modulated voice answered.

"Lois?" I asked.

"Yes," the tone was guarded.

"Donald," I said.

"Oh, you got my message?"

"Yes."

"I want to talk with you, Donald."

"Where?"

"I don't think we'd better try it in public. Could you come here to the Hillcrest Arms? It's apartment three thirteen."

"Is the coast clear?"

"I . . . I think so."

"I'll be there," I told her.

"When?"

"Within half an hour."

"That's good. I'm in a spot on account of—well, on account of you."

"I don't want that to happen," I told her.

"I don't either," she said, "but—I'll tell you when I see you."

"Okay," I told her, "I'm coming right up."

I made it to her apartment within fifteen minutes. I circled the block twice looking over the parked cars. I didn't see anything that looked suspicious, so I took a chance and went on up.

Lois had had class in her waitress' uniform and she looked even better in her street clothes.

She was the waitress for whom I had stepped back into booth thirteen, giving her a chance to get on by with the loaded tray. She had given me a brief smile and said, "Thank you, you're very considerate," and that was it.

She was in her late twenties with hazel eyes, chestnut hair.

"Donald," she said, "am I glad to see you."

"How did you find out how to get in touch with me?" I asked.

She laughed and said, "The information was forced on me, so to speak."

"By whom," I asked.

She smiled and shook her head. "There are only some things I can tell you. There are some things I hadn't better tell you, but I wanted to warn you."

"About what?"

"You're being framed for murder."

I smiled.

"Yes, you are," she insisted.

I said, "If it comes to an absolute showdown, I can get myself out, but that will mean pulling others in and I don't want to do it."

She made a gesture of impatience. "Don't be naïve," she said. "You think that you can bring in that police official who was having dinner with you. It won't do you a darn bit of good."

"Why not?"

"Because he's going to swear that he left there five minutes before the murder was committed, at least five minutes. The telephone call that his partner made is going to show a safe margin of time, and as far as the people who were dining there are concerned, the testimony is already all mixed up. They have two witnesses who will swear they saw Sergeant Sellers leave the table at least five minutes before the waitress screamed.

"You know what eyewitness testimony is. People think they see things that they don't. The police put ideas in a person's head; then they corroborate those ideas with testimony of another witness. The first thing anyone knows people are completely brainwashed."

"What's your part in all this?"

"I'm being brainwashed. I'm supposed to say that I bumped into you as you were coming out of booth thirteen."

"And have you told them that?"

"I have *not.*"

"What have you told them?"

"My story," she said, "is one they won't like."

"What is it?"

"It just happens," she said, "that I noticed you earlier in the evening when you were at the table. Babe, the waitress who was waiting on the man in booth thirteen, had pointed you out to me. She said that you were a professional detective and that you had helped Baffin out of a jam. I was interested in you and happened to notice when you left the room to take that telephone call. I saw you go directly to the lounge where the telephone is. Then, as it happens, when you were coming back, I was coming toward you with a loaded tray. You stepped back out of my way and in doing so stepped partially into booth thirteen. But you didn't go in.

"I thanked you rather . . . well, rather more than the occasion called for, although it was a nice gesture on your part. But I was— Oh, Donald, this is the damnedest thing for a girl to say, but you're in a jam now and I have to be frank. I was hoping that you'd . . . well, say something, be nice, you know.

"Anyhow," she went on, hastily, "I know that you went right to the telephone. I know that when you came back from the telephone, you went right to your table, except that you briefly stepped back into booth thirteen just long enough to let me pass. Your back may have parted the curtains a little bit but it was only your back. You never did face into the booth. You never did have the curtains parted all the way. You never were in the booth."

I said, "That's mighty nice of you and congratulations on your observation. That should take me off the hook."

"It should," she said, "but I don't think it will."

"Why not?"

She said, "You're bucking money and power and politics. Any one can be bad enough. All three could be fatal."

"Have you told them your story?"

"Not yet," she said. "I'm going to tell my story one

time and one time only, and that's going to be when I have publicity and protection."

"That serious?"

"Listen," she said, "I'm going to tell you something. It's something about Nick Baffin."

"Now, wait a minute," I said, "your job's at stake."

She looked at me incredulously. "My job!" she said. "Good heavens, do you think that's all that's at stake? I tell you *our lives* are at stake."

"What are you talking about?"

"I'm talking about the truth, the plain, simple, un-varnished truth.

"Baffin is mixed up with a man who describes him-self as a lobbyist—and that lobbyist in turn is tied up with a big-shot politician. They have lots and lots of money and they want to invest this money in legitimate business. Don't ask me why. I think they are afraid of some sort of investigation as to where the money is coming from."

"You've been reading books," I told her.

For a moment her eyes flashed. "I've been leading with my chin to try and protect a man that I thought amounted to something," she said. "Don't think I don't know what I'm talking about, I've been around and I've kept my eyes and my ears open.

"Three years ago Nick Baffin didn't have a dime that wasn't mortgaged for nine cents. Then all of a sudden he began to show signs of affluence. He seemed to have unlimited capital to develop his business. He started expanding. He opened a grill in Las Vegas. He opened one in San Francisco; one in Seattle. They're all of them the last word in style. They're all of them coining money.

"Now then, Mr. Detective, where do you think that money all came from at the start?"

"The syndicate?" I asked.

"This lobbyist. He may be a lone wolf."

"How do you know?"

"I was there," she said. "But I'll say this, the lobbyist looked up Nick Baffin. It wasn't the other way around."

"If you know this much about this lobbyist," I said, "he knows a lot about you."

She hesitated a moment, then lowered her eyes. "He knows a lot about me," she admitted.

"How much?"

"A lot."

"How much is a lot?"

"One hell of a lot."

"All right," I told her, "if that's the case he can put pressure on you. You can't afford to go against what he wants."

"It isn't a question of what I can afford, it's a question of what I'm *going* to do. And the first thing I'm going to do is to be unavailable for questioning. After all, I have to live with myself."

"How are you going to handle all this?" I asked.

She said, "They think I'm coming to work tonight, everybody does. I'm not going to show up. In an hour from now I'll be long gone."

"How long and how far?"

"Not very long," she said, "I can't afford it. I'm going down to Ensenada. I'm going to give myself a little vacation. I wanted to be in touch with you because I wanted to tell you where I'd be so you could reach me if you absolutely needed to.

"Now then, I'm going to tell you something else. This whole thing was some kind of a setup, and I don't know exactly what sort of a setup it was, but Calvert had a camera and was taking pictures of your party from inside that booth."

"How do you know that?"

"From Babe, the waitress who had booth thirteen."

"She's certain?" I asked.

"Not from what she told me, but from what I saw. I know Babe took a camera into that booth. The camera was on a platter and was covered with a silver cover, but underneath that silver cover was a platter with a camera on it."

I said, "Look, if you're going to get out, get out! This thing is getting too hot. You know too darn much."

"I have that feeling myself," she said. "I—"

"Are you packed up?"

"All I'm going to take. I don't want to take too many clothes. I don't want it to appear that I've deliberately run away."

"Get your things together and let's go," I said.

"Where?"

"Ensenada."

"You mean you'll put me aboard a bus?"

"I'll take you to Ensenada," I said.

"Wouldn't that undermine the value of my testimony? Wouldn't it look as though we had been . . . well, away together?"

I said, "Right now I'm thinking about your life. You've been thinking about mine; I'm thinking about yours. We're playing around with dynamite. Here, let's get started."

She went to the closet, took out a closed suitcase, said, "Now I only need to pack a handbag."

"Do it," I told her.

She put a handbag on the bed, busied herself with the contents of the bureau, then smiled at me. "Ready," she said.

I grabbed the suitcase and handbag and escorted her down to the agency car.

I pulled away from the curb, made a figure eight around the block, made an illegal U-turn, came to the conclusion no one was following me, and headed for the Mexican border.

Chapter 11

Driving down the congested coast boulevard, I said, "Now we have a chance to talk. I want to know something."

"What?"

"Why you are willing to quit your job, why you are willing to cut into a store of savings which I gather is rather slender in order to help a perfect stranger who—"

"You don't need to go any further, Donald. I have to live with myself."

I didn't say anything.

"Donald, do you think I could be part of a plant; that I could be playing a game?"

"No."

"Why don't you think so?"

"Because I like the look in your eyes."

"Okay, Donald, that's why I— Well, that's part of the reason I fell for you the way I did."

"All right, now we've got a breathing spell. Tell me about Calvert's camera."

"Babe seated him in the booth, took his order and then went back to the booth with another tray. I saw her at the serving table. She had a camera with a great big lens. She put it on the platter, slapped a cover over it and took it into booth thirteen."

I said, "There was no camera when the body was discovered."

She shrugged.

I said, "It impressed me at the time that the lighting on our table was exceedingly brilliant. . . . What about Calvert? Do you know anything about him?"

"No, I've seen him once or twice around the Grill, but I know very little about him really."

"Do you have any idea what this is all about?"

She said, "There was— What do you know about Morton Brentwood?"

"Not very much. He's a big-shot lobbyist tied in with one very important political figure, and I know one of the gossip columns said Brentwood was facing a quiz by the income tax people."

"All I know," she said, "are the names I hear plus what I read in the paper, but I know that there was a conference in San Francisco on the night of the fifth which lasted until the small hours of the morning. Brentwood was there. Nicholas Baffin was supposed to have been there. He told me afterwards that he didn't make it, but I think he did.

"Anyhow, a reporter for a San Francisco newspaper claims that a hundred-thousand-dollar slush fund was subscribed to support certain legislation."

"The evening of the fifth and the morning of the sixth," I said thoughtfully.

She nodded.

"That," I said, "could explain a great deal."

"Donald," she said, "you're mixed up in something big. We both are. You'll have to be very, very careful."

I nodded. "What happened to Calvert's camera?"

"Heaven knows. What happened to Calvert? Somebody got in that booth and out."

I said, "Thinking it over, I've come to the conclusion that the whole dinner was a plant. Our table was reserved right in the center of the room and under the bright lights. Calvert was placed in booth thirteen.

"That was the booth that was closest to the table and right in line with it. I think he was supposed to get pictures. The more I think of the manner in which our table was arranged, the more certain I am that that was what he was there for.

"The silver bucket with the magnum of champagne in it was on that side of the table. Frank Sellers was where his face would show in the pictures. There were bright lights overhead. Baffin suckered my partner and myself into making a setup.

"Calvert was working with Baffin—and he may have been working for somebody else on the side.

"Those pictures were important to someone. It was an elaborate setup to get Calvert armed with photographs.

"Then something came up all of a sudden which changed the picture. Someone else crashed into the act. . . . Any ideas?"

"None. I can't find any of the girls who saw anyone go into booth thirteen."

"I'm going to drive you only to Santa Ana," I told her after a while. "You can cross the border under your own power. Take a bus to Ensenada. Let me know where you are.

"Do it by sending me a postal card. Don't sign the postal card with your own name. Use any name you happen to think of. I'll understand."

She glanced sidelong. "You're not going down to Ensenada with me?"

"The more I think of it, the more I know it would be wrong. If I cross the border with you, they'll claim I was resorting to flight to avoid arrest and hold me on that charge."

She sighed. "I was hoping you could be down there with me—for a while, at least. It's going to be lonely down there."

"You may not have to stay there over a day or two," I said, "and there's just a chance I might join you later."

"Donald! Would you?"

"I don't want them to claim that I resorted to flight in order to avoid arrest," I said.

"I don't want you to take *any* chances," she said.

I drove her to Santa Ana, parked the car. "Here you are," I told her.

She held up her face for a goodbye kiss.

Chapter 12

When I called Elsie that afternoon she was in a panic.

"What's the trouble?" I asked.

"Those police," she said.

"What about them?"

"Frank Sellers demands that you get in touch with him."

"Lots of people want me to get in touch with them."

"Bertha is screaming her head off."

"Bertha usually screams her head off."

"Frank Sellers said I was to leave a message for you."

"What's the message?"

" 'In California, flight is an evidence of guilt.' "

"Who's fleeing?" I asked.

"He says you are."

"Look, Elsie, will you do something for me?"

"Of course."

"This is something pretty serious."

"I'd do anything in the world for you, Donald. You know that."

"Bertha is in and out?" I asked.

"Yes, Bertha is out quite a bit of the time."

"The next time Bertha goes out," I said, "put a message on her desk. Say that I called and wanted to talk with her; then when I heard she was out I said I'd call back in five minutes. That I called back and when she was still out, I told you I couldn't wait any longer. Are you willing to do that?"

"Of course."

"Bertha will ask you where I am, where I called from. You'll tell her that I was calling from a pay station; that I'm out working on an important case; that I just don't dare to let things go because the leads are too hot."

"All right," she said, "I'll tell her. Now, here's something else, this newspaper man, Colin Ellis, has called you three or four times. He says that it's very important that he get in touch with you."

"Okay," I said. "If he calls again tell him that you relayed his message. Tell him I'll get in touch with him within an hour."

"Donald, wouldn't that be terribly dangerous?"

"It'll be dangerous if I don't," I said. "Once the police get me in a position where they can claim I have resorted to flight, they'll be able to push me around.

"That leaves me no choice. I've got to see someone casually and in the course of routine business. Colin Ellis may be the best person on earth."

"He'll notify the police, won't he?"

"I don't think so. Ellis wants a story. If he can get the right kind of story out of it, he'd turn me over to the police and make a big bang out of the newspaper getting me to surrender myself.

"If he can't get the right kind of story or if I can string him along, he'll play for the *big* story.

"Then, when, and if it comes to a showdown, I can subpoena him as a witness and he'll have to admit that he was in touch with me all along."

"But if you tell him not to let anyone know where you are and—"

"That's the one thing I *won't* tell him," I said. "I'll tell him I'm working on a case and that things are happening so fast I just don't dare to be interrupted. I'll tell him that I've tried to get in touch with the office and talk with Bertha, but she's been out when I have called."

"Donald, that's terribly risky."

"In the position I'm in," I told her, "everything is terribly risky."

"Can I do anything to help? Anything at all?"

"Just what I've told you, Elsie."

"I'll do it," she said.

I hung up and drove the agency car around to a parking place from which I could see the front door of the newspaper offices where Ellis was employed. I knew his habits quite well and knew that he buttoned up his column about four o'clock in the afternoon; then went out for a couple of drinks and started going around picking up tidbits here and there, circulating through the bars and the night spots.

All of the night spots wanted publicity in his column and saved up everything they could for him about the comings and goings of important people.

Some of that stuff he published; some of it he discreetly withheld and some of it he didn't dare to publish. Taken by and large, Ellis knew more about the inside of things than almost anyone I knew.

At four-thirty Ellis came out and went into his favorite bar.

I went over to a telephone and called the newspaper office. "Colin Ellis," I told the operator.

"He is out at the moment."

"When do you expect him back?"

"I can't tell exactly. He's gathering material for his column. Can I take a message?"

"Yes," I said. "Tell him Donald Lam called."

"Oh, Mr. Lam," the operator said, "he's been trying to get you half a dozen times today. He's very anxious to get you."

"But you don't know when he'll be back?"

"I— No, I don't know just when he'll be back. Where can he reach you?"

"It's going to be difficult," I said. "I'm like he is, I'm gathering material. I'll try and contact him."

I hung up, waited five minutes; then strolled into the bar.

Colin Ellis was standing at the bar, getting an earful from the bartender and toying with a tall glass.

"Hello, Colin," I said. "My secretary told me you wanted to get in touch with me. I called you at the office, but—"

"Donald Lam!" he exclaimed. "Damned if I don't *really* want to talk with you."

"I'm listening," I told him.

"Buy you a drink," he invited.

"Same as you're having," I said.

"A Tom Collins."

"Suits me."

Ellis nodded to the bartender. The bartender fixed me a Tom Collins.

"Let's go where we can talk," Ellis said when my drink had been served.

I said, "Okay," picked up the glass, and we walked over to a booth at a far corner of the cocktail lounge.

"Now look, Lam," Ellis said, "let's be fair about this thing. You're in a jam."

"Me?" I asked, raising my eyebrows.

"You."

"How come?"

"A couple of witnesses are going to identify you as

emerging from that booth thirteen in Baffin's Grill just before the body was discovered.

"Now then, the police want to question you about it and there's no sense in trying to avoid the police."

"Who's avoiding the police?" I asked.

"You are."

"Not me," I told him. "I'm working on a case. I'm in communication with the office."

"Hasn't Frank Sellers been trying to get you?"

"Hell's bells," I told him, "there have been telephone calls from a dozen people who want to get me. If I played around with them, I never would get the job done that I'm working on and I'm working on one hell of an important job.

"I don't know what Frank Sellers wants but I'll talk with him when I get caught up, and I'm not going to talk with him before."

"Were you in booth thirteen at Baffin's Grill?"

"Don't be silly," I said. "I was called to the telephone. I came back to my table, and a waitress with a loaded tray came through the narrow passageway between the table and the curtained booth. I backed away to let her go by. I stepped back against the curtains of booth thirteen, but I didn't go in the booth and never was in the booth."

He shook his head. "You can't prove it," he said. "And a couple of witnesses *saw* you coming *out* of the booth."

"The witnesses are crazy," I told him. "What the

hell's the idea, somebody trying to frame me or something?"

"I wouldn't know," he said, "but if I were in your shoes I'd get in touch with the police right away and tell them my story."

"I can't do it right now."

"Why not?"

"Because I'm too busy."

He said, "The paper would go a long ways to back you up if you'd play ball with the paper."

"Play ball in what way?"

"You and I'll take a ride down to police headquarters. We'll get an ace reporter to go along with us. I'll handle it in the column. The reporter will handle it in the paper. We'll take a photographer along."

"You mean the paper will surrender me to the police?"

"Don't be silly. I said we'd give you a fair deal. You would come to the paper to tell your story. You'd learn for the first time that the police wanted you officially and we'd go see the police."

I said, "*You* were there at Baffin's Grill, what did you see?"

He said, "I saw you and your partner, Bertha Cool, having dinner, and I saw Frank Sellers."

"Did you," I asked, "see Frank Sellers leave?"

"Why did you ask that question?"

"I understand," I said, "that he had an important phone call."

"You should know. You're the one that gave him the message."

I didn't say anything.

After a while, he said, "Aren't you?"

I said, "As I understand it, Frank Sellers' story is that he left before the murder was discovered."

"Is that your story?"

"I haven't told my story yet."

"Is that why you're avoiding the police and publicity?"

I said, "Get it through your head, I'm not avoiding the police. I'm a working man and I'm on a job that's highly important."

He toyed with his glass. "Personally, I think you're playing a pretty deep game, Lam. I hope you don't get in over your head."

"If I get over my head," I said, "I'll swim. And if I don't get over my head, I'll wade."

"You folks had champagne," Ellis said.

"That's right."

"You had a magnum."

"Uh-huh."

"Was Sellers drinking with you?"

"Weren't you watching?" I asked.

"I was watching," he said. "I didn't notice particularly but I thought Sellers was bending an elbow right along with the rest of you."

"What does Sellers say?"

"He isn't available for interviews."

"You mean he's resorting to flight?" I asked.

Ellis threw back his head and laughed.

I said, "If anybody tries to pin anything on me, I've got the best alibi in the world."

"What alibi?"

"I got up and went to the phone," I said. "I was called to the telephone."

He nodded.

I said, "Frank Sellers' partner, Gillis Adams, says he called me to the telephone because he didn't want to page his partner. He made a record of the call; according to the police electric time clock that call was just four minutes before the murder was discovered."

"Well?" Ellis asked.

I said, "If I was talking with a police officer on a telephone, I couldn't have been in booth thirteen sticking a knife in somebody's back."

Ellis regarded me thoughtfully. "*Were* you talking with Gillis Adams?" he asked.

I said, "I'd prefer not to make any statement until I make it to the police."

"All right," Ellis said, "you win."

"On what?"

"All the way along the line. You've crowded me into a corner. I'm going to put cards on the table."

"Shoot," I said.

"Your partner, Bertha Cool, backs up the official police story," Ellis said.

"That's nice," I told him.

"She says that Frank Sellers was there, that he wasn't drinking, that you were called to the phone, that you came back and told Sellers his partner wanted him at the office at once on a most important development in the case they were working on; that Sellers jumped up and ran; that the murder wasn't discovered until several minutes after Sellers had left, that Gillis Adams met Sellers and the two of them were out working on this case until the small hours of the morning, that neither one of them knew anything about the murder in Baffin's Grill until after they wound up the night's activities and got back to headquarters."

"That sounds very reasonable," I said.

"The point is that the witnesses who saw you coming out of booth thirteen, or thought they saw you coming out of booth thirteen, are positive that it was less than fifteen seconds from the time you emerged from the booth that the waitress went in with the grub and started screaming."

"Witnesses aren't infallible," I said. "They get things mixed up all the time. You know that."

He said, "All right, Lam, now let's talk turkey."

"Dressed and cooked?" I asked. "Or strutting around in the raw?"

"Cold turkey," he said.

"Then it's been cooked," I told him.

"It's been cooked," he said, "but I don't know the answer, not yet."

"Why?"

"Look," he said, "the police in this city are in a vulnerable position right at the present time. The chief is pretty well entrenched, but there have been a couple of scandals. One more scandal would raise merry hell.

"Frank Sellers is a good officer, but he's rough. There's nothing diplomatic about him. He doesn't give a damn whose toes he steps on. When he wants something, he gets it. He has enemies.

"Now then, *if* Sellers had been sitting at your table and drinking, *if* he didn't leave until *after* the murder had been discovered, *if* this alibi that he fixed up with Gillis Adams can be cracked, and *if* Frank Sellers ducked out on that murder case because he'd been drinking a bit of champagne, and *if* he deliberately fixed up a fake alibi to get himself off the spot, there's going to be hell to pay."

"Yes," I said, "I can see that."

"Your partner, Bertha Cool, backs up the story Sellers told, but there's a time element in there that doesn't quite connect up."

"Why not?"

"You know why," he said. "Sellers left *after* the murder was discovered. There was a general exodus of guys and dolls who didn't want to be mixed up in the thing, but Sellers was smart enough to get the full implication just as soon as someone started screaming, 'Murder.' "

"What makes you think that?"

"I don't think it," he said quietly; "I know it."

"How do you know it?"

"Hell, I was watching," he said. "I saw Sellers hesitate over the champagne. Then he took a glass; then he had another glass. After that he was bending his elbow pretty frequently— Well, that's all right, he's not supposed to drink on duty and, in his position, he's more or less on duty twenty-four hours a day, but people won't hold that against him too much.

"But when it comes to ducking out on a murder case, building a fake alibi, trying to make you a Patsy so you'll have to support his story, things are getting pretty damn serious."

I looked innocent.

"Now then," Ellis went on, "I'm like you; I can jump either way on this story. I can back up Sellers' version and Sellers will be indebted to me for the rest of his life, or I can jump the other way and have one whale of a story which will result in a shake-up in police circles.

"I wanted to talk with you because I wanted to find out which way you were going to play it. It makes a difference with me."

"What am I supposed to say," I asked innocently, "that it makes a difference with *me* how *you* are going to play it?"

Ellis toyed with his glass. "You're one smart bastard, Lam," he said at length.

"What about Baffin?" I asked. "How does he sit on the sidelines through all this?"

"He doesn't."

"What do you mean, he doesn't?"

"I've got a whale of a story," Ellis said. "I can't publish it yet because I can't get the proof. But it's a hell of a story just the same."

"What kind of a story?"

"It involves you and it involves Baffin."

I raised my eyebrows.

"And," Ellis went on, "it involves Calvert, the guy who got himself murdered."

"It must be quite a story," I said.

Ellis sat closer and lowered his voice. "Baffin," he said, "was having hard luck up to about three years ago; then all of a sudden he branched out. He put in elaborate new fixtures, he became prosperous."

"Is that a whale of a story?" I asked.

"Of course not," Ellis said. "What happened is the guy got in with Morton Brentwood, and Brentwood's money financed him. There are lots of people who are wondering where all of Brentwood's money comes from."

Ellis went on, "Now, I know something I can't prove, but I think it's true. Calvert blackmailed Baffin for ten grand. It was a phony blackmail. Baffin put up the money that Calvert got on the blackmailing deal, and Calvert turned the money back to Baffin, all except a couple of grand he was permitted to keep."

"Why the blackmail?" I asked.

"Because something happened in San Francisco when Baffin was there. There's been a leak. Someone is just waiting to blow the lid off, but in order to do it they have to prove that Baffin was there. And if Baffin can prove he wasn't there, the whole thing would blow up. .

"That's the deal with Baffin. He was told to fix an alibi. He decided to do it by blackmail."

"Sounds interesting," I said.

"Then something happened," Ellis went on, "and Calvert wouldn't stay put. Calvert either knew what was happening, or else had made some copies of photographs that Baffin didn't know anything about, and Calvert was going to go to Baffin's wife. Baffin's wife has been wanting a divorce, but she wants alimony a lot more than she wants her freedom.

"Now, if this whole mix-up got into the divorce courts, Brentwood would either wind up having Mrs. Baffin get a chunk of the property, or he'd have to show that Baffin was a figurehead and that would mean that Brentwood's connection would have to come out in the open, and certain people don't want that.

"Now then," Ellis said, "I'm sitting on that story. It's a whale of a story, but I've got to have names, dates, telephone numbers, facts and figures before I dare to even think about publishing it."

I nodded. "I see your point."

"You," Ellis said, "can supply the corroboration."

"Me?" I asked, appearing to be startled.

"Don't act so damn surprised," he said. "you're playing a deep game— Now, I want to know which way you're going to jump on this thing because it makes a difference to me."

I shook my head. "You're getting me way out beyond my depth," I said.

"Then you'd better start swimming," he said, "because if you stay in where you are you're going to drown . . . and I'm the only life jacket you can rely on.

"Start thinking that over, Lam. If I have your corroboration, I think I can nail that story down.

"If you don't have my backing, they're going to frame you for the murder of Calvert—unless you back up Sellers' story. And if you're going to back up his story, I want to have the inside track on it. My paper wants to be the—"

I saw his eyes suddenly widen with surprise, then narrow in concentration.

Before I could turn, a hand came down on my shoulder.

Sergeant Sellers said, "Okay, Pint Size, I guess you and I have a little talking to do at headquarters. Okay?"

Ellis said quickly, "Gosh, you got here in record time, Sergeant."

"What do you mean, record time?" Sellers asked.

"From the time I telephoned you, of course," Ellis said. "The paper is turning him in and we want the story."

"The paper's turning him in, hell!" Sellers said. "I located the guy by putting out an all-points bulletin with the license number of the agency car he was driving. Knowing Bertha Cool as I did, I knew she was too tight to let him park the car somewhere and use a rented car to drive around in. However, just to be on the safe side we checked all of the rental agencies."

"What the devil are you talking about?" I asked.

"*You* know what I'm talking about," Sellers said.

Ellis got to his feet, said, "Now look, I don't want to have any misunderstanding about this. The paper sure as hell notified the police."

"When?" Sellers said.

"Just a short time ago," Ellis said. "When Lam walked in, I tipped the bartender off to call police headquarters, ask for you and tell you that Lam was here, that I thought he was going to let us surrender him to the police, but that in the event he didn't, you'd better drop around here and sit in on the conference."

"I never got any such call," Sellers said.

Ellis got up and started toward the bartender.

"No, you don't," Sellers said. "Call the barkeep over here and let me ask him what you said."

Ellis raised his voice. "Sam, did you make that call to police headquarters and ask for Sergeant Sellers?"

There was a half second of awkward silence, then the bartender said, "Sure thing, Mr. Ellis."

"What happened? Didn't you get Sellers? He says he didn't hear from you."

"The line was busy. That is, my line was busy," the bartender said. "Then when I got a line through, Sellers was out. I said the message was for Sellers personally. They said he'd be in about any minute, and

I asked them to leave a message that he was to call here."

"Call here?" Ellis asked.

"That's right."

"*Call* here?"

"Sure—you know, come here personally," the bartender said, picking up the cue fast.

Ellis walked back and sat down.

Sellers looked at Ellis, then at me. After a while he said, "What kind of a story you want, Ellis?"

"I want a story," Ellis said. "I want to show that Donald Lam knew he was wanted for questioning by the police; that he came to the paper and said that he'd like to have some protection and asked if the paper would see that he got a square deal if he turned himself in. The paper said that it would."

"You don't need any newspaper to get a square deal from the cops in this city," Sellers said.

"I'm not talking about what *we* said. I'm talking about what Donald said."

"You publish any story you damn please," Sellers said, "only Donald and I are going up to headquarters, and we're going to have a nice little talk."

"And I'm coming along?" Ellis asked.

"You're staying right here." Sellers said. "You've got a story to write. Only when you write that story, don't let it appear that I came here because of any notification from you. I came here because of good, old, solid, substantial police methods. I put out an all-points bulletin for Lam's car. An officer picked it up in the parking lot across the street. I figured he'd be in here and—here I am."

Ellis turned to me. "Donald, are you going to tell the story of—"

"Donald isn't going to tell you any story," Sellers said. "We're investigating a homicide. We want our investigation confidential for the time being. . . . Come on, Pint Size!"

He twisted his fingers in the collar of my coat, half lifted me to my feet.

"We're in a hurry," Sellers said. "You haven't any more time to waste in conversation."

"Donald," Ellis asked, "can I have your confirmation on the story?"

"Shut up!" Sellers said. "Come on, Lam, we're going places."

He hustled me out of the bar.

Chapter 13

The room at police headquarters was a typical sweat-box.

The brown linoleum on the floor was drab and streaked with what seemed to be black caterpillars. Actually these were the residue of nervous suspects who had discarded lighted cigarettes while under the impact of police interrogation.

Sometimes the police will let a suspect smoke, but they seldom provide him with ash trays.

The scarred, battered surface of the table also had quite a few of these black caterpillars of varying length. The lone window in the room was barred. The door had a spring lock. The chairs were hard, durable, uncomfortable, the relics of a bygone era in furniture making.

There was nothing else in the room, just table and chairs.

I sat in a chair at the head of the table. Gillis Adams, Sellers' partner, and Frank Sellers sat on each side of the table.

Sellers said, "You know when I left the Grill you gave me the message that Adams here gave you. I left right away, didn't I?"

"Right away after what?"

"After you gave me the message."

"Did I give you a message?" I asked.

"Now look, Lam," Sellers said, "you're at the forks of a road. You either play ball or you don't play ball. Now, tell me about the message you gave me."

"I'll tell my story on the witness stand," I said.

Sellers scraped back his chair, got to his feet, and stood over me threateningly. "You smart-aleck son of a bitch, I've put up with all I'm going to stand from you."

"The whole story," I said, "on the witness stand."

Adams said, "Now, wait a minute, Frank, let's not jump at conclusions. Maybe the guy's all right."

"You were having dinner with me," Sellers said.

"That's right."

"You had liquor?"

"Yes."

"And I wasn't touching any, was I?"

I said, "I'll tell my story on the witness stand."

"You'll tell it here and now," Sellers said, "and you'll sign a statement."

I shook my head. Sellers pressed a button on the table. Almost immediately the door was opened from the outside and a man in uniform said, "Ready any time you are, Sergeant."

"Come on, Pint Size," Sellers said. "*We'll* show *you* something. Then you can do a little thinking."

They took me into another room, opened a door, escorted me across the room and Sellers opened another door, said, "Okay, boys."

Five boys came shuffling in. Two of them were in jail uniforms. Two of them were obviously cops. One of them had the nervous twitching of a dope addict.

"This way," Sellers said, and opened another door.

We went through a passageway into a shadow box.

This was a long, narrow boxlike structure with lights along the edge and a gauze curtain over the front.

Lights came on and we were blinded by them. We couldn't see a thing beyond the gauze curtain which was brilliantly illuminated by the lights, but we could hear voices.

A voice from the outside gave orders. "All right, men, take two steps to the right."

We took two steps to the right.

"Back two steps to the left."

We walked back two steps to the left.

There was a period of silence.

I heard Sellers' voice saying, "Can you make an identification?"

A feminine voice said, "Certainly, the second one from the right-hand side."

"You mean the one in the middle?"

"That's right, the one in the middle. There are three on his left, two on his right," the feminine voice said.

"You're positive that's the guy?"

"That's him. I'll swear to it."

"How about you?" Sellers asked.

Another feminine voice said, "There's no question about it. That's the man."

A door opened. "All right," an officer's voice said. "File out and into this room."

We filed out of the shadow box. An officer held another door open and the five men went out, leaving me in the room.

Sellers came in, and after a moment, Gillis Adams.

"Well, you heard it," Sellers said. "You've been identified as the man who was coming out of booth thirteen shortly before the murder was discovered. . . . I guess that does it, Pint Size."

I didn't say anything.

"Now let *me* tell *you* something," Sellers went on, "you haven't burned any bridges, not yet, but now you know where you stand.

"Baffin came clean. He was being blackmailed by

this Starman Calvert. He agreed to pay him ten grand, because Calvert had the goods on him for a night he spent at the Restabit Motel with a dame.

"Baffin came to you. You paid the ten grand and got the pictures, the registration card, and the rest of it, but you got cagey and wouldn't turn the evidence over to Baffin—probably because you had blackmail ideas of your own. I don't know what you had in mind, but Baffin thinks he knows.

"Anyway, you got a statement from Calvert that he was a blackmailer; that he had received ten grand in return for evidence, and you took the evidence and apparently are still holding it.

"Now, we want that evidence, and that statement.

"Calvert was a blackmailer and if it weren't for the fact that Baffin has a perfect alibi, we'd suspect him, but so far you're the prime suspect."

"What's Baffin's alibi?" I asked.

"He was talking with Morton Brentwood. The two men had been together for half an hour before the waitress discovered the body—for at least ten minutes before Calvert walked into booth thirteen. They remained in discussion until the headwaiter came rushing in, his face all pasty, and said there'd been a murder."

"I see," I said.

"Now then," Sellers went on, "Brentwood is in a jam. Some people who are hostile claim that he was at a meeting in San Francisco on the evening of the fifth; that a couple of other people were present; that Brentwood persuaded them to contribute to the slush fund for certain legislation.

"Not that that isn't all right and perfectly legal *unless* you can read 'forced' for 'persuaded.' "

"So Brentwood came down here to ask Baffin if he'd deny being there. Is that right?" I asked.

"Brentwood," Sellers corrected, "came down here to see if he could find *proof* that Baffin wasn't in San Francisco at all that weekend, but was down here.

"Baffin isn't particularly eager to show where he was or what he was doing, but he can do it if it comes to a showdown."

"Then that's where I came in?" I asked.

"That's where you come in," Sellers said.

I didn't say anything.

"Now then," Sellers said, "where are the photographs?"

"The photographs," I told him, "are in a safe place."

"Baffin wants them."

"Baffin wasn't my client. I redeemed the photographs for somebody else."

"All right, we want them," Sellers said. "They're evidence."

"Evidence of what?"

"Of the fact that Calvert was a blackmailer."

"You know that already," I told him.

"Now look, Pint Size, we're not fooling around here swapping words. If you want to come through, now's your chance."

"And if I don't?"

Sellers grinned. "We're not going to make an arrest, not just yet, but we are going to let it be known that you've been identified in a line-up by two people who saw you coming out of booth thirteen shortly before the murder was discovered."

"Very attentive witnesses," I said. "Did you inquire of them whether you had been drinking at the party, and whether you left before or after the waitress dropped the tray of dishes?"

Sellers face darkened. "You smart-aleck bastard, I could—"

"Hold it, Frank," Gillis Adams said, "the guy's been identified in a showup."

"Some showup," I said, "I was the only one in there that looked like me."

Sellers grinned. "We thought it was a very fair showup. The men were all very similar to you in age, build and appearance."

"Phooey," I said. "Two of them were jail inmates. Two of them were big cops."

"Then name them," Sellers said.

"Hell, I don't know their names."

"Then you can't prove very much, can you, Pint Size? It's just your word. . . . I thought it was a very fair line-up, didn't you, Gillis?"

"Gosh, yes," Gillis said, "I thought it was exceptionally fair. Of course, we had to work fast, but we just put him in a box and the girls picked him, both girls."

"One girl, after she had heard the other make an identification," I said.

"I don't think she heard," Sellers said, "I was talking in a low voice, but it doesn't make any difference."

"What am I supposed to do now?" I asked.

"You've been busy working on a case."

"That's right."

"Your partner, Bertha, wants to see you."

"I've been trying to get in touch with her."

"Try it again," Sellers said.

"You're not holding me?"

"Hell, no," Sellers said, "we're just investigating. You're free as the air. Only when we get some more evidence against you, we'll pick you up again and if we get a little more evidence than that, we'll put you in the gas chamber."

"You think you can get any more evidence?"

"Oh, I'm sure of it." Sellers grinned. "We can get lots of evidence. We've really got enough already, but we're just trying to be absolutely certain, you know. We always want to give a prisoner the benefit of the doubt."

"So I can go on about my business?"

"Sure, sure," Sellers said.

"Only," Gillis Adams said, "you're supposed to be a bright guy. You'd better start doing a little thinking."

"About what?"

"About everything."

Gillis got up, walked across the room and opened the door.

I walked out.

Chapter 14

I left headquarters, picked up the agency car and drove directly to the office.

Elsie Brand's jaw sagged when she saw me coming in the door.

"For heaven's sake, Donald!"

"What's the matter and why are you working late?"

"I thought you were . . . well, you know, the police."

"Elsie," I said in the patient tone one uses in instructing a rather backward but entirely lovable child, "I told you that I wasn't resorting to flight. I told you that I was just busy working on a case."

"I know," she said, "that's what you *told* me."

"And I wouldn't lie to you, would I?"

"I didn't think it was a lie, I thought you were trying to protect me so I wouldn't get into trouble for compounding a felony or something, or aiding you in trying to escape."

"Give it no thought," I said. "Bertha's been looking for me?"

"That's the understatement of the week."

"Is she in?"

"Yes."

"Okay," I told her, "I'll go see what Bertha has to say."

I walked out of my private office, across the reception room and into Bertha's private office.

She looked up with eyes that were glittering with hostility. "Where the hell have you been?"

"Working."

"I wanted to talk with you the worst way."

"I couldn't seem to get a good phone connection," I said.

"Well, you didn't try very damn hard."

"All right," I said, "I'm here now—the phone I used must have been out of order. . . . What's the pitch?"

She said, "Frank Sellers wants to see you."

"Oh, yes, good old Frank," I said. "I've already seen him."

Her face softened. "Have you, now?"

"That's right."

"Then it's all fixed," Bertha said.

"What's all fixed?"

"Sellers wanted to see you before you made any commitments."

"Well," I told her, "I haven't made any commitments."

"Oh, that's fine, Donald. I was afraid we couldn't depend on you."

"What do you mean 'we'?"

"Well, you know—sometimes you get old-fashioned ideas about honesty and ethics."

"What," I asked, "are the modern ideas of honesty and ethics?"

"Now, don't be sarcastic," she said.

"I was just asking."

"We're no longer hypocrites, we're practical. The modern idea is that we're living in a competitive world and we have to make a living under conditions which will stand up competitively."

"And when you translate all that double-talk, what does it mean?"

"Fry me for an oyster," Bertha blazed, "don't be so goddam dumb!"

"I'm just trying to get your thinking in my perspective."

"Well, you'd better enlarge your perspective then," she snapped.

"To include what?"

"To include the fact that we are backing Frank Sellers up one hundred per cent."

"In what?"

"In his story."

"And what's his story?"

"You know what his story is. He's going to have to tell it sooner or later. So far, he's managed to duck telling it where it counts.

"He was with us. We were drinking. He wasn't drinking. He joined us at dinner at our invitation because we had something we were going to talk over with him. His partner, Gillis Adams, knew where he was because Sellers has to keep in touch with headquarters at all times.

"Adams wanted to get in touch with Sellers on account of a very important development in a case they were working on, but he didn't want to have Sellers paged publicly. So he decided to call you, particularly in view of the fact that he had reason to believe you were known to Baffin and that Baffin had passed the word on down along the chain of command to see that you had everything you wanted and that it was all on the house.

"So Adams asked to have a waiter go and call you and have you come to the phone. Then when you came to the phone, he told you to tell Sellers to get to headquarters at once without even stopping to phone for instructions, that it was terribly important.

"You went back to the table and gave the message to Sellers, and Sellers bolted for the door. Now, all that was *before* the waitress dropped the dishes and made the scene, and before anybody had yelled 'Murder.' "

"And Sellers wasn't drinking," I asked.

"Not a drop," she said.

"Why not?"

"Because officers aren't supposed to drink when they're on duty, and a man in his position is on duty twenty-four hours a day. Of course, that's largely a fiction, and after they leave headquarters for home, they indulge in a drink now and then. But I'm talking about the regulations in his particular department. . . . At our table you and I were drinking champagne and Sellers was drinking pale ginger ale in a champagne glass."

"You've told that story?" I asked.

"I've told that story," she said.

"You're going to continue telling it?"

"I'm going to continue telling it, and so are you!"

"Someday you're going to have to tell it under oath."

"All right, then, I'll tell it under oath."

"And that might be perjury."

"Prove it's perjury," Bertha snapped. "Damn it, Donald, do you realize that we're in business here; that if we have the ill will of the police, we can't continue in business; that all we need to do is just be a little broadminded and we can help Sellers out of a bad spot and Sellers won't forget it?"

I said, "We help him out of a bad spot by committing perjury and then something happens and it turns out we've told a lie and the murderer slips through the fingers of the district attorney because of that lie and then all hell breaks loose. Instead of just covering up for Sellers, we've been mixed up in letting a murderer get turned loose and then we lose our license; Sellers gets fired and maybe you get prosecuted for perjury."

"Horsefeathers!" Bertha snorted.

"Did you," I asked, "notice the cigar and cigarette girl?"

"What do you mean?"

"You remember the girl who was going around in the tights, with the low-cut bodice with the tray of cigars and cigarettes?"

"Sure, I remember her," Bertha said. "She was all but naked above those ballet tights."

"All right," I said, "Frank Sellers wanted a cigar. She bent over to light it for him. His eyes were doing a double take.

"That girl doesn't sell many cigars in a place like that. Her sales are mostly cigarettes. So suppose she remembers Sellers, and maybe kept her eye on him. Then what?

"I tell you, Bertha, we can't stick our necks out until we know a lot more about the people who are keeping quiet.

"How about the big exodus, the people who couldn't afford to be seen there? Someone will uncover these people, or some of those people. That will be a later development. What will they testify to? We can't afford to take a position at this time.

"We don't know who committed that murder, when it was committed or why it was committed, but before long the answers may come out. The time element may prove to be very important.

"If Sellers tells the truth and says, 'Sure, I was sitting there having a party with Donald Lam and Bertha Cool because I heard Baffin had been blackmailed and I wanted to find out about it, and the only way I could find out about it was to be sociable. So I was there. Then somebody yelled, 'Murder,' and people started stampeding out of the place and I felt it would be a mighty good thing for a police officer to be down at the sidewalk level getting a line on the people who came out so we could remember them later on. I went down there and was as inconspicuous as possible, but I didn't see anything worth while.'

"Now, if Sellers tells a story of that sort, there's enough truth in it so he isn't going to open any doors for the murderer; the district attorney isn't going to get sore at him for throwing monkey wrenches in the machinery, and, what's more important, nobody can blackmail him.

"But the minute you and Sellers get on the stand and start swearing that Sellers had left before that commotion took place in the booth; then the real story becomes highly important, a perfectly priceless piece of blackmail. Not for money, perhaps, but to hold Sellers in line any time anybody wants to crack the whip."

Bertha's eyes started blinking rapidly.

"Fry me for an oyster," she said, after a moment.

She thought things over, then reached for the telephone, thought better of it and moved her hand back.

"You see what I'm talking about?" I asked.

"I see," she said. "I think you and Sellers should have a talk."

"To hell with talking with Sellers," I said. "Sellers is batting my ears back, and Sellers is planning to charge me with that murder. If he can come up with the real murderer, that's okay with him. If he can't, he's going to pin the murder on me. And under those circumstances I'm going to protect myself every way I can."

And while Bertha was thinking that over, I opened the door and walked out.

Chapter 15

I waited until I was certain that Baffin would be at the Grill; then drove up to the Baffin residence, parked my car, walked boldly up the front steps and rang the bell.

A maidservant answered the bell.

"I want to see Mr. Baffin," I said.

"He isn't home."

I raised my voice. "It's quite important that I see him. I have been employed by Mr. Baffin to report on certain things and I want to get in touch with him."

"He isn't here. He's at the Grill. You had better try to reach him there," the maid said.

"Oh, thank you!" I said, started away, then turned and came back. "It's rather inconvenient for me to meet him at the Grill. I'd like to meet him privately. What time do you expect him home?"

"Oh, he doesn't come home until late. He's at the Grill until one or two o'clock every morning."

A woman's low, well-modulated voice said, "That's all, Vera. I'll handle this."

I looked up and saw Mrs. Baffin smiling at me. "There was something you wanted?"

"Yes, I wanted to see Mr. Baffin, but I didn't want to see him in a place as public as the Grill. I thought perhaps I'd catch him before he left."

"No, he leaves quite a bit earlier. . . . What did you want to see him about? I'm his wife. You can talk to me."

I acted self-conscious. "I'm afraid it's a private matter."

She said, "Well, come in, anyway, and we'll see if we can work something out."

I hesitated, then followed her into the living room. "Drink?" she asked.

I smiled and said, "No, thank you. I'm on duty, in a way."

She said, "You're doing some work for my husband, aren't you?"

I thought that over and then said guardedly, "Well, you might call it that."

"I'm his wife, you know."

"Yes, I know."

She took the bull by the horns, smiled seductively,

crossed her knees and said, "And I know who you are. You're Donald Lam. You're a private detective. You are part of the partnership of Cool and Lam."

I pretended great surprise.

Her voice was cooing and seductive. "Donald, did my husband employ you to spy on me?"

I shook my head emphatically.

"What was it he hired you to do?"

"I don't think I should discuss it—that is, I think you'd better ask him about it, Mrs. Baffin."

"Then there's been some development?"

"Yes."

"What?"

"Well," I said, "you must know all about it because it's been in all the papers."

"Oh, you mean the murder?"

"Yes."

"You've found out something in connection with that?"

"Well, in a way, yes. I wanted to talk to Mr. Baffin about it."

"You don't think you should discuss it with me?"

I hesitated and said, "I don't think so."

"You've got a new lead and a new clue?" she asked.

I said, "Well, in a way, yes— Perhaps I can tell you about it after all."

"Oh, I wish you would, Mr. Lam," she said. "I get terribly bored sitting here by myself every evening. You know, my husband has to work afternoons, evenings and until one and two o'clock in the morning every day, and it leaves me— Well, you know the old song, 'A Bird in a Gilded Cage.'"

"A beautiful bird," I said.

She lowered her eyes demurely. "Thank you," and hitched the hem of her skirt down a sixteenth of an inch, calling attention to the shapely knee and the smooth nylon stocking.

I said, "The big thing in chasing down a murderer is to find out everything one can about the victim, his friends, his enemies, the persons who might have had a motive for the killing."

"Yes, I can understand that."

"Now, in the case of Starman Calvert, no one seems to be able to uncover a motive—"

"Have you thought of blackmail, that he might have been a blackmailer?" she asked.

"Oh, yes," I said, "I've thought of it and I think perhaps that's right, but it takes quite a powerful motive for a person to commit a murder.

"However, what I was going to say was that no one seems to have been able to contact his wife, as yet."

"I understand. The poor woman."

"That," I said, "would be tragic if it weren't suspicious."

"What do you mean, suspicious?"

I said, "Suppose his wife wasn't really his wife, but a woman with whom he was living undercover. She masqueraded as his wife. She wore dark glasses nearly all the time. She was a beautiful blonde—just about your age and build, but a woman who was seen only on a few rare occasions."

"But that's because she was traveling as a purchasing agent for a department store."

"The department stores say no."

"Does it have to be a department store here? Couldn't it have been a department store in Chicago or San Francisco?"

"San Francisco says no. I don't think they've tried Chicago. She'd hardly be working for a department store in Chicago and living here."

"Why not? She was in and out, and she was out more than she was in. After all, this is the age of the jet plane."

"Yes," I said, "there's something to that."

There was silence for a few seconds, then she said, "Well, you've got something you wanted to tell my husband?"

"Yes."

"About her?"

"Yes."

She stiffened to attention. "What is it, Donald?" she asked, lowering her voice so it was a confidential half-whisper.

I said, "The woman *masqueraded* as Mrs. Starman Calvert. She had a credit card as Mrs. Calvert. I found where she bought her gasoline and used her credit card. I've got a really good description. The attendant saw her without her dark glasses. He can identify her."

"Indeed!" she said. "Where is this service station?"

I became cagey. "That's what I wanted to tell your husband."

She thought a moment. "You have a description?"

"Almost a photographic description," I said.

"The poor woman," Mrs. Baffin said. "Imagine the spot she's in. Heavens, she may be some respectable married woman living with her husband and this will blast her reputation and ruin her life."

I looked thoughtful. "It could be," I admitted.

"I'll tell you what, Donald, just forget about seeing Nicholas on this, and when he gets home I'll wait for just the right opportunity and tell him. I'll tell him that you have the clue that you think will enable you to run down this Mrs. Starman Calvert, and that there is now evidence that she may have been some married woman who was leading a double life."

"I don't like holding out on Mr. Baffin," I said, "in a matter of this sort."

"You're not holding out on him. You've reported to me. Mr. Baffin is busy up there running the Grill, and I happen to know he has a thousand-and-one important things on his mind and he just doesn't want to be disturbed. I'll tell him when he gets home."

"Thank you," I said, and stood up.

She smiled. "Now then," she said, "having discharged your duties, how about that drink?"

I hesitated, then said, "I still don't think I should, Mrs. Baffin, but thanks a lot."

She pouted. "I was hoping you'd say yes—after all, it's pretty monotonous sitting here alone. I don't want to take up knitting, and I'll be damned if I'll have a cat, and I . . . well, I get lonesome."

"I can understand," I said. "I'm surprised you . . . well . . . never mind."

I averted my eyes.

She came to stand close beside me.

"It's been so long since I've had anyone take me out to dinner, hold my chair at the table, show me the customary little courtesies—sometimes I think I'm going mad, absolutely mad, sitting out here alone, night after night, watching television. If I don't dress up, I start getting seedy, and if I do dress up all I do is sit in the living room and look at my reflection in the mirror across the room. . . . Donald, when I cross my legs, do you think I show too much?"

"No."

"The mirror indicates that I do."

"The mirror has a lower point of view than a person would have."

"I didn't shock you, did I, Donald?"

"You interested me."

"You think I have pretty legs?"

"Beautiful."

"Oh," she said, giving me a playful little slap, "You're nothing but a flatterer."

I laughed and said, "And I'll bet you use that line with all the men who tell you have pretty legs."

"There aren't so many men—these days."

"That," I told her, "is a crime."

"And my husband is paying you to prevent crime, isn't he?"

"In a way, yes."

"Do you have to go, Donald?"

"Yes, I've got work to do. I'm still on the job."

She sighed. "All right," she said, "but remember."

"Remember what?"

She laughed. "Remember me," she said, and escorted me to the door.

Her eyes followed me down the steps. There was no panic in them.

The car that was parked in front was a Thunderbird with a different license. Nick Baffin was probably driving the Cadillac.

Chapter 16

I got a sandwich, a thermos bottle of coffee, a package of cigarettes and drove up to a parking place where I could keep watch on the service station where Mrs. Calvert had bought gasoline.

I settled myself for a long wait.

I needn't have bothered. I hadn't been there thirty minutes before Mrs. Baffin drove up in the Thunderbird.

She was her seductive best. She got out of the car, went to the restroom; returned and chatted with the attendant while he was filling the car. She stood close, smiling up at him, and all in all, was there for nearly ten minutes having the tires checked, the battery checked and all the time engaging in conversation.

When she had left, I crossed over to the attendant.

"You again," he said.

"Me," I told him.

"Find that credit card that had been stolen?"

"I think so," I said. "What about the woman that was just in here with the Thunderbird?"

"Her?"

"That's the one."

"What are you talking about?"

"I want to know about her."

"A heck of a nice woman, courteous, considerate, refined, and—"

"She use a credit card?"

"No, she paid cash."

"No idea who she was?"

He shook his head. "I've never seen her before."

"She wanted information?"

"Oh, she's like all these women. They read about a murder and get all hepped up about it. She wanted to know if I'd ever seen Calvert, and pointed out that his apartment was not too far away. Then she asked about Mrs. Calvert, my ideas about her, and all of that. She asked me if Mrs. Calvert traded here, and I told her I couldn't remember all my customers, but I thought I'd seen Mrs. Calvert's name on a credit card a time or two, but those credit card customers were just names to me. I couldn't remember what they looked like from the credit cards, but if I'd see them again I'd know I'd waited on them.

"This dame was curious all right—but in a nice sort of way."

I said, "All right, here's what I want to know. Is there any chance, any possible chance, that this woman you were talking with is a woman who has traded here often?"

He looked at me in surprise. "Hell," he said, "not a ghost of a chance."

"Thanks," I told him, and drove off.

Mrs. Calvert had used Baffin's car on at least one occasion. She was thirty-two or thirty-three and blonde, and for the most part, wore dark glasses day and night. What I had said had started Nick Baffin's wife on a hot scent.

And the fact that Mrs. Calvert and Nick Baffin's wife weren't one and the same woman had dashed my theory of the case into a thousand pieces and left me out on the end of a limb.

I estimated I had about twenty-four to thirty-six hours before anybody lowered the boom on me. Provided, of course, I kept lucky and kept in the middle of the road.

I picked up a phone and called Baffin.

He was terribly agitated.

"Lam," he said, "I've simply got to see you. I have a job for you."

"What kind of a job?"

"A big job this time."

"Is this your job, or is it—"

"No, no, it's my job. I want you to come around here to my office just as quick as you can get here—provided you're free to move. Are you free?"

"Free as air," I told him.

"I'm in my private office. How soon can you get here?"

"Fifteen minutes."

"Make it ten if you can," he said. "Money is no object. This thing is terrible—simply terrible."

"Be seeing you," I told him, and hung up.

I sensed it might be a trap, but in my position at the moment I had to keep the ball rolling. I took a chance.

Baffin was in his sumptuous private office on the second floor. There were dark circles under his eyes. He looked like hell.

"Lam," he said, "I don't like you."

"That's a good beginning," I told him.

"You did, however, stand on principle. You went against your own interests in maintaining a loyalty to a person who is only technically your client. They say you're smart. I'll take their word for it. I know you're loyal. I need to buy loyalty."

"How much loyalty?"

"All you have to sell."

"What do you want?"

"I'm going to tell you a story," he said.

"Shoot," I told him.

Baffin said, "I'm going to have no misunderstandings this time. I'm going to retain you to protect *my* interests."

"What are your interests?"

Baffin moistened his lips with the tip of his tongue. "They're going to frame me for murder," he said.

"Whose murder?"

"Calvert's."

"How come?"

"Do you know Morton Brentwood?"

"I know of him."

"He was with me when Calvert was murdered, but someone's brought pressure to bear on him. The way he remembers it *now* he was talking on the phone to San Francisco for about ten minutes."

"Where from?"

"In the phone booth right outside this office, but he now says he had his back turned. I *could* have gone out."

"Did you go out?"

"Certainly not!"

His eyes wavered.

"Did you go out?" I asked.

"I did step just outside the office for thirty seconds. Brentwood was in the phone booth. His back was half turned, but he should have seen me going out and coming back."

"You *were* out?"

"Yes, for not more than half a minute."

"What time was this?"

"About five or ten minutes before the scene in the restaurant."

"You mean when the waitress discovered Calvert's body?"

"Yes."

"What do you want me to do?"

"There are some things you can't cover up, particularly in a murder case," Baffin said. "Too many people can put two and two together. Word has got around that Calvert was blackmailing me."

"Tell them the truth," I said. "Tell them that it was a frame-up."

"Oh, that part of it is easy," Baffin said. "It's the second part that bothers me."

"What's that?"

"The story that Calvert was going to go to my wife and give her copies of the pictures."

"He'd made extra copies?"

Baffin nodded.

"How did you know?"

Baffin said, "The son of a bitch wanted twenty-five grand."

"Did you kill him?"

"No, I wish I had."

"Do you know who did?"

"No."

I said, "If you killed him, I'm going to get you convicted, because I'm going to find out who committed the murder."

"I didn't kill him."

"And you're positive you don't know who did?"

"Right."

"All right," I told him. "I want to bring a little pressure to bear."

"On whom?"

"The murderer—and if you're the murderer, the pressure is going to be on you. I want that understood right at the start."

"It's understood."

"All right, I want to get some color pictures and have them processed almost at once. I know a photographer who can do the job. I want you to furnish the models."

"What models?"

I looked at my watch.

I said, "There's a Japanese camera with a fast lens, I mean really fast. The lens has a rated speed of f 0.95.

"Now, who was the waitress who was waiting on Calvert, the one who discovered the body?"

"Babe," he said.

"All right," I said, "get Babe on the job, get an order of Chinese food cooked up. I'm getting a camera. Keep the second floor closed to all customers until I get the pictures I want."

"What are you going to do with the pictures?"

"Use them for window dressing," I said. "Make me a check for a thousand dollars. I'm going to get the camera and make arrangements to have the films developed. I'll be back in twenty minutes. I want you to have things all ready."

I went to the camera store that was open evenings

where I had seen the new fast-type lens, bought the camera and a roll of color film. I was back at Baffin's in just under twenty minutes.

"Everything set?" I asked.

"Everything is set," Baffin said.

"Let's go," I told him.

We went out and met Babe.

Babe was a beautiful blonde with a nice figure, come-hither eyes, and an air of assurance about her.

Baffin performed the introductions.

She looked at me and said, "What do you want?"

I said, "I want you to fall and spill food all over the floor."

She averted her eyes. "Again?" she asked.

"Again," I said.

"That was a horrible mess. I—"

"I'll have the busboys clean it up," Baffin interposed. "Do what Lam wants."

"Yes, Mr. Baffin," she said.

"And," I said significantly, "keep quiet about it."

She nodded.

I saw that the lights were turned on bright in the center of the room.

"Let me focus the camera," I said.

While I was focusing the camera, I took three pictures of her. The shutter was so quiet she didn't even hear it. Then I had her pose with the tray, took a picture of the tray falling to the floor, and afterwards a picture of the resulting mess with Babe lying there on the floor.

"A little more leg," I said.

She pulled up her skirts.

"Whoa, back up, that's too much. This isn't for a girlie magazine. It's a news photograph."

She pulled her skirt back down and said, "Just tell me what you want."

"A little more."

She raised the skirt slowly, provocatively.

I clicked the shutter three or four times, bracketing the exposure.

"Okay," I told Baffin, "get the boys to clean up the mess, say nothing to anyone, and keep Babe quiet. Can you control her?"

"Heavens, yes."

"Okay," I told him, "start controlling her then. I want her to forget all about this."

I went to the laboratory where I had made arrangements to process and print the color film and helped the technician for two hours. At the end of that time, I had some very good color shots.

I put in my wallet one print of the waitress spilling the food and put the rest of the prints in an envelope, marked the envelope, "Donald Lam, personal, confidential," put on the office address, sealed the envelope and dropped it in the mail.

I called Elsie's apartment and checked with her.

"What's new at your end, Elsie?"

"Nothing."

"Nothing at all?"

"Nothing. Everything is quiet."

"That's good," I told her.

"No, it isn't," she said. "It's the quiet that precedes the storm. You can just feel it in the air. Even Bertha is walking on tiptoes."

"And there's been absolutely nothing new?"

"Not a thing— Oh, wait a minute, somebody sent you a telegram from Ensenada."

"Who?"

"There was no name on it."

"What kind of a message, Elsie?"

"Just a message saying good luck and signed Casa de Mañana."

"That's fine," I told her, "forget all about it. It's some idea for an ad, a motel trying to drum up business for weekend parties."

Chapter 17

I left well before daylight so that I was down in Ensenada bright and early.

The office of the Casa de Mañana said they had a Lois Malone stopping there and I went around and tapped on her door.

I didn't get any answer until the second knock.

"Who is it?" she asked.

"Donald," I said.

She hesitated a moment. "The last name?"

"Lam."

"Just a minute," she said.

I heard feet on the floor; then the door was opened. She was standing there in a robe, her hair tumbled about her neck.

"Well," she said, "*you* certainly give a girl an opportunity to look her best when you come calling!"

"You look all right to me," I told her.

"What's cooking?" she asked. "What brings you down so early in the morning?"

I looked up and down the long passageway.

"Come on in," she invited.

I entered the room, a typical high-class motel bedroom with the bed rumpled but the room neat and clean, the clothes all hung in closets with the exception of some nylon underthings on the back of the chair.

She started to grab those; then looked at them and laughed. "I guess you've seen things like that before, Donald. Sit down. I was lying here reveling in the luxury of being able to sleep as late as I wanted."

"I have an idea it's about time to go back and face the music," I told her, "unless the music comes down here and faces us first."

"Nobody has even given me a tumble so far."

I said, "I'm leaving a back trail."

"Why?"

"Because," I said, "I want to be sure that they can't pin flight on you."

"What do you mean?"

"If you fled, it would indicate a guilty conscience, and in California flight is an evidence of guilt. If, on the other hand, you were a material witness and I stashed you away, that's something else."

"So you left a back trail?"

"I'm driving the agency car," I said. "It's registered. The officers have found me once by putting out an all-points bulletin on that car and they can do it again pretty easy if they want to. If they don't find us, we've got the record of my having been here."

"What are you going to do?"

"Register. Stay here all day. Drive back tonight."

"You go and do that, Donald," she said, "and give me a chance to take a shower, clean my teeth, and get presentable. I feel all fuzzy."

"Breakfast?" I asked.

"Half an hour."

"You have a place?"

"I'll tell the world I have a place. Not here, where they have hot cakes, ham and eggs, but a cute place where they have huevos rancheros, papaya, and wonderful mangoes."

"That's for me," I told her. "I'll be back in half an hour."

I registered at the motel under my own name, gave the license number of the agency car, waited half an hour; then went back to pick up Lois.

She was a trim package, long-legged, streamlined, healthy, normal, clear-eyed.

"How much does Nicholas Baffin miss me?" she asked.

"He hasn't said a word about you being gone—not to me."

Her eyes narrowed slightly. "That's significant," she said.

"It's interesting," I told her. "Let's eat."

We ate. We went swimming. We loafed on the beach in the sunlight. We rented a motorboat and went riding around the bay and out in the ocean, then we brought the boat back and took a long walk down the beach.

After a while, we came to a place where sand dunes, brought in by the wind, were piled up white as chalk, soft, warm and tempting with slopes that caught and reflected the sunlight, valleys that held shadows.

We lay on the sand dunes. Lois, with her head on my shoulder; then down on my chest, her arms around me. She slept peacefully.

After a while, I dozed off to sleep. I wakened when I felt her shifting position, and then opened my eyes to find her studying my face. There was a tender smile on her lips. Her eyes were blinking back tears.

"Now what?" I asked.

"Nothing," she said, "except I'm—"

"So you start crying?" I asked.

"Uh-huh."

"Why the tears?"

"I'm just happy I've known you and unhappy I didn't know you sooner, and . . . and I'm worried."

"About what?"

She said, "As long as they don't know what my story is, as long as I'm in a position to get on the stand and swear that you didn't come from booth thirteen, that you simply stepped back against the curtains to let me pass, they can't frame you for murder without having the whole thing backfire.

"However, if I should be . . . well, let's say, unavailable—you know how the police work. They'd brainwash the witnesses; they'd find witnesses who were favorable; they'd find witnesses who wanted to curry favor with the police. Well, you know what would happen."

I shook my head. "They couldn't prove me guilty beyond a reasonable doubt. They might frame up a case that would enable them to arrest me, but that would be the extent of it."

"Don't fool yourself, Donald," she said. "If I were out of the way . . ." She smiled at me. "I'm your life insurance."

I nodded.

She kissed me, a long, clinging kiss; then pulled her head back twelve inches, looked me in the eyes and said, "So, take good care of me, Donald."

The shadows lengthened. We walked back up the beach and had a good dinner.

"You're staying over?" she asked, and it was more of an invitation than a question.

I shook my head.

Her face showed a quick cloud of disappointment.

"I've done the job I came down here to do," I told her. "They can't say either one of us resorted to flight now. If I can get back without attracting attention, I've got the registration down here and the receipt for my room to show that I was investigating a case."

"And," she added, "that takes me off the hook. By the same token, I'm a witness that you have stashed away instead of a suspect fleeing the authorities."

"It works both ways," I told her.

"Couldn't you leave tomorrow morning?"

"Not very well," I said. "I'd better go while the going's good."

She took a deep breath and smiled. "All right, Donald," she said, "you know best."

Her good-night kiss was deep and tender.

I drove as far as the border before I was picked up.

The highway patrol said, "We have a bulletin on your car. Let's see your driver's license."

I gave him the license.

"Aha," he said, "wait here. I've got some telephoning to do."

He went into the phone booth and was gone for about ten minutes. Then he came out and said, "Which way you going, Mr. Lam?"

"I'm headed for my residence in Los Angeles."

"Where have you been?"

"South of the border."

"How far?"

"Ensenada."

"Doing what?"

"Interviewing a witness."

"To what?"

"A matter I'm investigating."

"You could be a little more co-operative. It might cause you less inconvenience."

"And it might cause me more," I said. "I'm paid to gather information, not to broadcast it."

"You're a private detective?"

"You saw my card. You've got the registration of the automobile. You know what you wanted—or rather what somebody else wanted."

"When did you go down to Ensenada?"

"Early this morning."

"How early?"

"Real early."

"We were looking for you on the way down. You weren't running away, were you?"

"If I was," I said, "I wouldn't be coming back. You can mention that in your report if you want."

He thought things over, said, "All right, Lam, you may go. There's no charge against you. We're just checking, that's all."

I drove on. For an hour nothing happened, then a motorcycle officer sirened me to the curb.

Once more I showed my driver's license.

The California highway patrol officer was courteous, efficient and somewhat apologetic.

"There's a pickup on you, Lam, from Los Angeles County. You're wanted for investigation in connection with a murder."

"You going to arrest me and leave the car standing here?" I asked.

"No, I am not," he said. "I *could* take you into custody, but I don't think that's necessary. However, I'm going to let you drive your car and I'm going to follow you. I'm also going to radio the Los Angeles police that I'm escorting you in."

"Fair enough," I told him. "I can't keep you from patrolling the highway right behind me if that's what you want to do."

He grinned and said, "That's what I want to do."

We moved fast along the road. When I got to Los Angeles, Frank Sellers was waiting for me with a squad car.

"Okay, Lam," he said, "you can consider yourself detained for questioning and investigation in connection with that Calvert murder."

"Okay by me," I told him. "You've got the authority. If you want to use it, go ahead, but I just warn you, Frank, you're making a mistake."

"Save your warnings," he told me. "You had your chance to co-operate. Now you can try taking it on the chin for a while and see how it feels."

We went to headquarters. Sellers took me to the booking desk and said to an officer, "Search him."

The officer went through my pockets, having me turn each pocket inside out.

They took the envelope from the inside pocket.

"What's this?" the officer asked, looking at the color picture of Babe dropping the dishes.

"Hey!" the officer said to Sellers, "I think we've got something here, Sergeant! I think this picture ties in with that case we're investigating."

Sellers grinned from ear to ear. "He's a smart canary," he said. "He could be trying to hold out a little something on us.

"What have you got there, Pint Size?"

I shook my head and said, "No comment."

Sellers grinned, took out the picture, looked at it, frowned and then suddenly his mouth dropped. "Son of a bitch!" he said under his breath.

"Isn't that the waitress that found the body?" the officer asked.

Sellers closed his eyes, concentrating on the problem. At length he said, "How the hell do I know? It looks like her."

"We can find out," the officer said. "If somebody had a camera there, we'll find out who it was and get all of his pictures. A set of pictures could show lots of things."

I looked at Sellers and caught the sudden flash of panic in his eyes.

I grinned.

Sellers said to the officer, "This guy is ringed with luck and he's a daring and diligent investigator. If anybody had a camera in that grill, this is the little son of a bitch that *would* locate the guy and get the pictures."

He turned to me. "Where did this picture come from, Lam?"

"No comment," I said. "I'm protecting my sources of information."

Sellers hit me hard in the stomach. "We don't let private dicks protect their sources of information when we're working on a murder case. Where did that picture come from?"

I was feeling a little squeamish, but I put on quite an act. I staggered around, gagged a couple of times, doubled over, fell to my knees, groped around on the floor.

Sellers kicked the seat of my pants hard.

I lunged forward and lay still.

An officer hurried up to Sellers and said something in a low voice, cautioning him.

Several men who were being booked looked at the show sympathetically.

Sellers, his face livid with rage, said, "Get up, you pint-sized runt, and you're going to tell me where you got those pictures or I'll skin you alive."

I staggered to my feet, looked him in the eye, and said, "If you *want* those pictures, I'll see that the *whole roll* is published. Perhaps that will suit you!"

Sellers started to say something, changed his mind, took a good long look at the picture, said, "Take him in and lock him up."

I was escorted down a corridor into a cell which had

a washbasin, a toilet, and two bunks. The odor of jail disinfectant permeated everything.

I was alone for about fifteen minutes; then Sellers came in. He also was alone.

"I'm sorry I lost my temper with you, Pint Size," he said.

"Go to hell," I told him. "I think you've ruptured my liver."

"Hell, I just gave you a little poke to get your attention," Sellers said. "That wasn't a blow."

"I want to see a doctor."

Sellers started to get mad all over again, then brought himself under control. "All right, Donald," he said, "you can see a doctor if you think you're hurt. We haven't anything against you right at the moment that I'm going to hold you on, but I don't like you shooting down to Mexico."

"Why?"

"I told you you were under investigation. I don't like to have people run away."

"I wasn't running away. I was running back."

"Where did you get that picture?"

I shook my head.

"If someone was in there with a camera, that's evidence," Sellers said patiently. "That's the highest type of evidence. You know what happens to persons who conceal evidence." Sellers went on, "Now look, Lam, you and I are on opposite sides of the fence but that doesn't keep us from being friends."

I didn't say anything.

"I have to know about that picture."

"What about it?"

"It's evidence."

"Evidence of what?"

"Evidence of—well, it shows that waitress dropping the tray."

"All right," I said, "it shows the waitress dropping the tray. What does that mean? That doesn't have anything to do with the murder or the murderer. It simply has to do with the waitress. There's no question about the identity of the waitress. There's no question about what she did when she pulled back the curtains of the booth and looked inside. The murder was all over by that time. The murderer had escaped and the picture has no evidentiary value. The district attorney couldn't introduce it in court."

"I'm not sure about that," Sellers said. "I want to find out about that picture. I want the original."

I shook my head.

Sellers leaned forward and grabbed me by the shirt and the lapels of my coat. He jerked me toward him. "You little bastard," he said, "you try to hold out on me and I'll turn your face into hamburger."

"You big bully," I retorted, "you try to push *me* around and I'll see that the whole damn string of pictures is published. Were you drinking champagne, sitting at the table, gawking with your mouth open while people were discovering a murder?"

"You double-crossing, son of a bitch," Sellers roared, "that's a hell of a way to treat anybody who's tried to stick up for you."

"Yeah," I said, "I know the way you stick up for me. My stomach hurts. I want to see a doctor. I think my liver is ruptured. You're a big, strong, brutal officer and you hit harder than you realize."

Sellers fished a cigar from his pocket, shoved it in his mouth, chewed on it savagely for a few seconds; then said, "All right, go ahead, get the hell out of here."

Chapter 18

I went to the office, retrieved the pictures I'd mailed myself, and found a message to get to Baffin's place as fast as possible. When I got there, Baffin looked at me with the helplessness of a trapped animal.

"Brentwood's suit for defamation of character against a San Francisco newspaper has been filed in San Francisco," he said.

I nodded.

"I'm going to be a witness," Baffin said.

"Testifying to what?"

"That I wasn't even in San Francisco at the time the claim was made that Brentwood was soliciting money under such circumstances that it amounted to a potential bribe. I was here in Los Angeles. That's what the blackmail was about."

"And you're supposed to testify to that?"

"Yes."

"And Calvert was supposed to testify to the blackmail?"

Baffin shifted his position and said, "If necessary."

"Now Calvert is dead. He can't testify to anything," I said, "and you're in a spot."

"What do you mean, in a spot?"

I opened my brief case and took out the photographs I had taken of my car parked in front of the Restabit Motel. "This photograph mean anything to you?"

He looked at it; then said, "It's very similar to the photographs that Calvert took of my car."

"Very similar indeed," I said. "Both photographs were taken deliberately and posed."

"You've said that before."

I said, "Now I'm saying it again. What's more, that blackmail picture is dated."

"What do you mean dated?"

"I mean you might as well have had the photographer put the correct date on the picture—Monday, the thirteenth, not Monday, the sixth."

"You're crazy," he said.

"Look at this picture," I told him, indicating the picture I had taken."

"What about it?"

"It was taken Tuesday, the fourteenth."

"So what?"

"See that apartment building going up next door?

See the line of girders just coming up in the background? Now, remember back to your picture. The skyline was almost exactly the same. The girders were just beginning to show.

"You forgot about that building going up. That puts a date and a time on your photographs just as though you had stamped it with a time clock.

"That ten-story apartment building is going up against a time limit and they're working their heads off trying to beat the time limit. There's a bonus of seven hundred and fifty dollars a day for every day the contractor can beat the deadline. The contractor can beat the deadline. The contractor wants that bonus."

Baffin thought that over. His face was a study.

"Now then," I went on, "we come to the murder of Starman Calvert. He was murdered in your place. There's this bit of blackmail hocus-pocus that you had with him.

"As long as he was a blackmailer who had been paid off by you so that there were no further demands, you didn't have a very strong motive for murdering the guy. But once he enters into a new aspect as a conspirator in this blackmail charge, you're out on the end of a limb. You're the number-one suspect."

"Why?"

"Because Calvert could have squealed on you."

"He had no reason to squeal."

"That's what you say—now."

"Well, if I could talk with Brentwood I'd have a perfect alibi. I couldn't have left here without him seeing me, while he was telephoning, he was in that booth just outside my door."

"He was talking on the telephone. He had his back to the door."

"Is that what he says?"

"According to the newscast I heard on the radio, he says he was standing where he feels sure he could have seen you if you had left the room. Get that, he *feels sure* he could have seen you. He doesn't say positively. He doesn't back it up with any iron-clad guarantee. It's just a matter of opinion. But you *did* leave the room briefly and he *didn't* see you."

"What are you getting at, Lam?"

"You've got to come clean," I told him, "otherwise you're getting yourself all tangled up."

Baffin ran a hand over his moist forehead. "What can I do?" he asked. "I'm trapped."

"You're not trapped," I told him. "You're in a spot, that's all. To begin with you can trust me. Now, Frank Sellers is going to be calling you and asking you about where I got a picture of the waitress, Babe, falling down in a half-faint, dropping the tray of dishes and screaming. He'll want to know how I located the person who had the camera and—"

"He already telephoned me about fifteen minutes ago."

"The hell he did!" I said. "What did you tell him?"

"I told him the truth. I'm not going to lie to the cops."

"You told him that was a posed picture?"

"Yes."

"That we posed it afterwards?"

"Yes."

"You damn fool," I told him, "that picture was my certificate of immunity from arrest. As long as I had them guessing about that picture, they didn't know which way to jump, and they didn't dare try to pin it on me. Now you've got your ace detective framed for murder—provided they don't blame it on you!"

I looked at the main exit from the office, then turned to a side door. "Where does this go?"

"Into a closet."

"Any exit from the closet?"

"Yes, you can go from the closet to a private stairway which leads to the kitchen. I keep an eye on things from the office and—"

I never heard the last of it. I was through the door, into the closet, down the stairs into the kitchen, and through the kitchen headed for the back.

I reached the alley which had a long row of sour-smelling garbage pails. I looked up and down the alley. It was a long way to the street.

I ducked back inside the kitchen. A Chinese cook was slicing onions.

There were two or three white caps and uniforms

hanging on a hook. I just pulled on a white cap, shoved my arms into a white uniform, walked up and began slicing onions.

The Chinese cook looked at me with a puzzled expression.

We heard voices. Frank Sellers said, "When I catch that guy, I'll throw the key away this time."

He came dashing down the stairs, threw one hasty look at the kitchen, saw the two of us working there, and stormed out into the alley.

I slipped the Chinese boy twenty bucks, slid out of my white uniform, beat it through the kitchen to the front door.

Sellers' squad car with the red light on and motor running was parked in front of the door.

I tried to make my appearance casual as I waved for a taxi to come up.

The taxi was slow getting started. Eventually it came up. I got in the cab. The cabby was just closing the door when Frank Sellers came barging out the front door of the restaurant. He tackled me like a football player tackling an opposing runner.

He had the handcuffs on me almost all in one motion.

"You fourflushing son of a bitch," he said. "You pint-size fourflusher. This time you're *really* in trouble!"

He hauled me out of the cab to the sidewalk.

A small crowd began to form.

Sellers manhandled me into the police car.

"You and your phony pictures!" he said.

"What's phony about the pictures?" I asked.

His laugh was short and sneering. "Wanting me to think you'd located someone who'd taken a whole set of pictures up there at the café."

"What the hell are you talking about?" I asked.

"What I'm talking about," he yelled, "is that phony picture. You had it posed."

"Sure I had it posed," I said. "I didn't tell you it was taken at the time of the murder, and I didn't tell you I had a set of pictures taken the night of the murder."

"No, you let me draw my own conclusions. You were a smart bastard. That's the trouble with you, you're smart. You're too damn smart! This time you've out-smarted yourself!"

I said with dignity, "I took that picture for a purpose. I wanted the subject to think that I was trying to dupli-cate the scene the night of the crime. I wanted Nick Baffin to think that's what I was doing. But actually I wanted the picture for another purpose. The rest of the pictures are in my inside coat pocket."

Sellers retrieved the pictures.

"Keep talking," he said. "It's music to my ears. I like to have you chatter, particularly when you've got all your teeth. After I get done with you, you might not have all your teeth."

I managed a yawn. Sellers was so mad he bit his cigar clean in two, threw the severed piece out of the car win-dow, said, "I know! You're like all these smart alecks, you think you're protected by a lot of laws and regulations that enable you to violate the law any time you want to, but if a cop so much as lays a finger on you, you scream of violation of your civil rights and want six attorneys and a lot of hearings before commissions and courts and what have you? To hell with you, Donald Lam, I've got news for you. In about fifteen minutes, you're going to resist an officer in the performance of his duties."

I didn't say anything.

Sellers was driving toward headquarters.

"Go on," he invited, "make some more with the chin music."

I said, "You're too dumb to be interested. You're just leading with your chin. Whether that photograph was what you thought it was or not doesn't alter the situation that you were on a drinking party when the murder was committed, taking a magnum of champagne on the house."

"It was Bertha's dinner," he said.

"Phooey," I told him, "Baffin wouldn't have given Bertha a sandwich. She was the decoy. *You* were the game he was after!"

I could see that jarred Sellers.

I said, "I wanted that picture because I wanted to get Babe, the waitress, to pose for a color camera shot and that was the only way I could do it. I let both Baffin and Babe think I was trying to duplicate what had happened the night of the murder. Actually, I was trying to get something I could use as a means of identification."

"Identifying who for what?" Sellers asked.

I said, "This Calvert murder is being handled completely backwards. You haven't a motive yet. You don't know anything about Calvert's background. You've been unable to find his wife.

"*I've* found his wife."

Sellers even took his eyes from the road for a flashing second. "You have?" he asked.

I nodded casually.

"Yes, you have," Sellers said, sarcastically. "This is some more bait you're putting on a hook, trying to catch me."

"Have it your way," I said. "You go ahead and solve the case your way, if you want to."

"Now look, wise guy," Sellers said, "I've let you talk me into things before."

"And," I told him, "you've always hit the jackpot in the long run."

"I've been lucky as hell," Sellers said, "I've listened to you and I've fallen in over my eyebrows; then I've crawled out smelling like a rose because of just plain damn luck."

"You think its luck," I said. "We sell that stuff up in our agency. Bertha calls it brains, and we make money on it."

I could see that Sellers was beginning to waver.

"What about this guy's wife?" he asked.

I said, "The woman who posed as Calvert's wife was—"

"Who *posed* as Calvert's wife!" he interrupted.

"Sure," I said, "she was a phony. Otherwise, she'd have come forward by this time, or you'd have found out about her. In fact, if you'd gone about it in the right way, you'd have found out about her by this time."

"Oh yes, smart guy," he said, "and what was the right way?"

"Credit cards," I said.

"What credit cards?"

"She had a gasoline credit card," I said. "She signed tickets for gasoline."

Sellers threw back his head and laughed. "And you thought that hadn't occurred to us? Hell, we've chased down those gasoline tickets. We have her signature. We have the license number of the automobile she bought the gas for. It was the one that was registered in Starman Calvert's name. Now then, what's so bright about *your* detective work? What do you know that we don't know?"

I said, "I have a ticket that you don't know anything about. It was a ticket she issued when she had a car filled that didn't belong to Starman Calvert."

"Who did it belong to?"

"Nicholas Baffin," I said.

"What?" Sellers shouted.

I didn't say anything.

Sellers slowed the car. "Now, listen, Pint Size," he said, "don't try to hold out any information on this thing. This is murder, and you start holding anything out and you'll *really* wind up behind the eight ball."

I said, "How far behind the eight ball can I get?"

Sellers thought for a moment, then grinned. "You've got a point there," he said, pulled the car into the curb and parked it. He shut off the motor, studied the set of color pictures, half closed his eyes, fished a new cigar from his pocket, started chewing on it.

After a moment, he said, "Now listen, Pint Size, I'm going to do some thinking. I want you to keep your damn mouth shut. I've listened to you and the siren sound of your honeyed words too long. What happened to this ticket?"

"I presume it's been sent in," I said. "I got a glimpse of it long enough to jot down the license number."

Sellers sat silent, suddenly he leaned forward, turned the ignition key, started the motor and said, "Where is this place?"

"What place?"

"The service station."

"Straight ahead," I told him. "Turn to the left at the second traffic light. It's quite a ways from the apartment where Calvert lived, but I just kept covering gas stations."

Sellers muttered, "Son of a bitch," under his breath, said nothing else.

I directed Sellers to the service station.

"Take the handcuffs off and I can be of more assistance to you," I said.

He said, "Shut up, Pint Size. I'm running this. We've had enough masterminding. This is going to be regular police stuff."

Sellers drove the car into the section and pulled out the leather folder with his badge and I.D. card.

"Police," he said to the attendant. "You seen this guy before?"

The attendant looked at me and said, "Sure, he was around checking credit cards. He's a private eye working on some lost card."

"Remember what cards?" Sellers asked.

"I've forgotten the name now. Something beginning with a C, I think."

Sellers took the photograph of Babe from his pocket, the one I had taken when she was standing straight and smiling against the curtain of booth thirteen.

"Know this dame?" Sellers asked.

The attendant started to shake his head.

"Take a *good* look at it," Sellers said.

The attendant narrowed his eyes, said, "Wait a minute. Wait a minute . . . yeah, I know her."

"Who is she?"

"I don't know her name," the attendant said, "but she's been in here once or twice with a credit card. I know that."

Sellers put the photograph back in his pocket, handed

the attendant one of his cards. "You see her again or think of her name or anything, you call me at headquarters. Okay?"

"Okay," the attendant said.

"Try and think of her name."

The attendant shook his head. "When we work with credit cards we just check the signature to see they correspond. Lots of times we take everything for granted."

"I know," Sellers said, "but sometimes things come to you."

"Uh, huh," the attendant said.

Sellers started the motor, swung the car in a U-turn. After a couple of blocks, he pulled in at the curb. He didn't say anything, but took the key from his pocket and slipped off the handcuffs.

Sellers drove rapidly to Baffin's Grill. He was chewing on his cigar steadily, fraying the end, then biting off part of the soggy tobacco and spitting it out of the window of the car.

He didn't say anything, and I didn't say anything.

At the Grill, Sellers parked his car, pushed his way through the door, said, "Come on," to me, and we went up to the offices on the second floor.

Baffin was there.

Baffin looked us over with some surprise.

"This girl named Babe, this waitress, where does she live?" Sellers asked.

Baffin shook his head. "You can search me," he said.

"What time does she come on duty?"

"Tonight's her night off."

Baffin looked from Sellers to me.

Sellers walked around the desk, grabbed a handful of Baffin's shirt, jerked him half out of the swivel chair, said, "You son of a bitch, *where does she live?*"

Baffin's jaw sagged open. "I— What are you—"

Sellers roared, "I said, 'Where does she live?'"

"I told you I didn't know."

"Try again. You're shacking up with this girl on the side. She has enough of an inside track so she can take your car on occasion when she wants it and drive around town in your big Cadillac. Now then, you tell me where she lives or you're going to the cooler."

"My wife—" Baffin said.

"To hell with your wife. This is a murder rap."

Baffin said, "Let me go. I'll get it for you."

Sellers threw him back into the chair, letting go of the hold he had on Baffin's shirt and necktie.

Baffin straightened his collar, reached in a desk drawer, took out a small black notebook, opened it to a page and handed it to Sellers.

Sellers gave the book a quick glance, closed it, put it in his pocket, said to Baffin, "Come on."

"I'm busy," Baffin said. "I have an appointment with—"

"I said, 'Come on'," Sellers roared.

Baffin slowly got to his feet.

"At this point," I told Sellers, "you need Bertha."

"At this point," Sellers said, "I don't need a damn thing except good old police methods."

"Have it your way," I said, "but the Supreme Court has changed some of *your* old-time police methods—remember?"

Sellers looked at me angrily. "Any time I need some smart runt of a private eye to tell me what to do—"

"That's now," I said.

"What's now?"

"That you need a private eye to tell you what to do. According to the Supreme Court decisions, if *you* uncover any evidence by what you call your good old-fashioned police methods, the exclusionary rule will tie your hands. But if some independent, private party uncovers the evidence, you, as a police officer, can take advantage of it. Surely, they've briefed you on that ruling of the courts?"

Sellers stopped dead in his tracks, blinked his eyes at me for a moment and said, "You think it'll work?"

"I think it will work," I said.

"Let's go get Bertha," he told me.

I jerked my thumb toward the phone.

Sellers said, "What's the number?"

I gave him the number.

Sellers called and got through to Bertha.

"We're going places, Bertha," he said. "I'll have a police car in front of your door in about seven minutes.

Meet me there. . . . That's right, down on the side-walk."

Sellers slammed down the receiver.

"Let's go," he said to Baffin.

Baffin said on the way down, "I can assure you of one thing, probing my private sex life isn't going to help you solve your problem."

"That's what you think," Sellers said. "I'm doing the thinking from now on."

Baffin turned to me angrily. "I hired you to protect my interests, Lam. This is the second time you've double-crossed me."

"Shut up, you goddam fool," Sellers said. "If this smart son of a bitch is playing the right hunch, he's getting you out of the biggest jam you were ever in in your life."

"And giving my wife the biggest alimony any lawyer could ask for," Baffin said.

"If you keep your mouth in just the right shape," Sellers said, "the police aren't going to go blabbing to your wife."

"What shape do I keep my mouth in?" Baffin asked.

"Shut," Sellers told him.

We got in Sellers' car, and Sellers drove as only a police officer can drive, but even so it was ten minutes before we picked up an impatient Bertha.

Bertha looked us over in surprise. The car heaved over on its springs as she hoisted herself into the front seat beside Sellers.

"What do you want, Frank?" she asked.

"Let that smart bastard tell you," Sellers said, jerking his head toward me.

I said, "Babe, the waitress who discovered Starman Calvert's murder, who was taking the food in to him in booth thirteen, is the long missing Mrs. Calvert, the bereaved widow whom the police have been looking for."

"Fry me for an oyster," Bertha said.

"What!" Baffin shouted. "Why the two-timing little—"

"Shut up, Baffin," Sellers said. "Go on, Lam."

I said, "A great deal depends on how she's handled. The police are under wraps with some of these Supreme Court decisions. They've got to give her a long rigmarole about her right to counsel at all stages of the proceedings. If they make a search and discover anything, they can't bring it into court unless they can show that the search was made under reasonable grounds. If a private citizen takes it upon himself to make the search and uncovers something worth while and the police are advised of what has been found by the private citizen, then the police have reasonable grounds."

"Who's the private citizen?" Bertha asked.

"You are," Sellers said.

Bertha grunted and settled herself a little more solidly in the car.

Sellers turned on the siren and off we went.

Chapter 19

We made a grim procession as we left the elevator and marched down the hall of the high-class apartment hotel.

Bertha Cool was marching on ahead. I came next, then Nicholas Baffin, the outraged cuckolded lover. Sellers, beginning to enjoy himself, chewing on a soggy cigar, brought up the rear.

Bertha held out her finger to jab the mother-of-pearl bell to the right of the door.

I grabbed her wrist and said, "I think Baffin can do better than that."

Baffin looked from one to the other of us.

Sellers said, "You heard the guy, Baffin. Do better than that!"

Baffin said, "What do you mean?"

Sellers said, "The key, you dumb bunny."

Baffin sighed, took a leather key container from his pocket and fitted a key to the lock.

We opened the door and walked in.

Babe was primping in front of the foyer mirror, wearing a robe and slippers.

She looked over her shoulder, saw Baffin, started to smile, then saw the rest of us and her mouth popped open in consternation.

I said, "We have some bad news for you."

"Bad news?" Babe asked, looking from one to the other, her jaw hanging slack.

"Yes, Mrs. Calvert," I said, "we wanted to let you know that your husband has been murdered. Police have been looking for you, trying to notify you."

"My husband—" she said.

"You two-timing bitch," Baffin said.

"Now, just a moment," Babe said, drawing herself up to her full height. "This is my apartment. I resent this intrusion of my privacy. I am entitled to consult a lawyer. I demand that you leave my apartment."

"Whose apartment *is* it, Baffin?" I asked.

Baffin swallowed. "Mine," he said.

Bertha turned to Baffin. "What do you want done with the apartment?" she asked.

Baffin struggled with disillusionment. "I want it vacated," he said.

Bertha said to Babe, "Get your things together, dearie."

"Who are you and what are you talking about?" Babe said. "You can't come into my apartment and order me around like this. I'm entitled to notice. I'm entitled to—"

"Got your rent receipt handy?" Bertha asked.

"And I don't have to take orders from you," Babe said.

"Oh, I'm just here to help you, dearie," Bertha said. "Come on, we'll help you pack."

And Bertha crossed the living room to the bedroom, opened the door and started looking in the closet.

Babe came at her like a flash. "You big bitch!" she exclaimed and grabbed for a handful of Bertha's hair.

Her hands never got home. Bertha gave her a stiff arm that would have done credit to a collegiate football player, then ducked inside, grabbed her around the waist and threw her half across the apartment.

By the time Babe smashed off the wall and caromed onto the bed, all the fight was taken out of her.

Bertha said, "Where did you get the knife that killed him, honey?"

"I . . . I didn't get it."

"But you killed him," Bertha said. "You got tired of him hanging around and—"

"Let's let *her* tell us about that, Bertha," I said. "I think it's a little deeper than that."

The robe had fallen off, and Babe was on the bed in panties and bra, looking at us with wide, frightened eyes and trembling lips.

"How much do you know?" she asked, her eyes on my face.

"By the time you've told us the answers to a couple of things," I said, "we'll know the whole story. You didn't know he was slated to die, did you, Babe?"

She shook her head, her lips quivered. "It was the d-d-d-damnedest shock I ever had in my life," she said.

I said, "Brentwood was in a jam in San Francisco. He had to show he was innocent of the charge they had made against him. He couldn't get out of it by himself, but he *could* get out if Baffin could show he wasn't in San Francisco on that date.

"So Baffin got Starman Calvert to hatch up a blackmailing scheme, got me to make the pay-off, the idea being that if any investigators started nosing around, I could be very hush-hush about it but could prove to them that Baffin actually was in Los Angeles on the fifth and sixth.

"They forgot about the skyline in that apartment house.

"That left Calvert in a position of holding the whip hand, and Calvert, like a damn fool, tried to pull a blackmail, a real blackmail this time, holding up Brentwood.

"Brentwood and the people he plays around with are the type who play rough. I don't know whether

Brentwood intended to kill him or not, but he came down here and had a conference with Baffin and then he went out, ostensibly to telephone.

"First he had me paged to be sure I'd not be watching what went on. Then he did the job he'd been planning, after giving me a warning on the phone.

"Actually he was gone about ten minutes, long enough to sneak a knife from the kitchen, enter booth twelve, stand on the banquette, lean over the partition and when he found Calvert sitting slightly forward with his chin on his palms he simply dropped the knife into his back. The heavy kitchen knife needed only a little extra force to penetrate to a vital spot.

"Then Brentwood reached down, lifted the camera, went back to the telephone booth and . . ."

"And left *me* holding the sack," Babe finished.

"You got anything besides chin music to show for all this?" Sellers asked me.

"I wonder if *you* have?" I asked Babe.

By way of answer, she went over to a drawer, pulled out a letter, which said,

Dear Babe:
We can't go on like this. I think Nick is getting suspicious. I made a couple of grand over that fake blackmail he staged, but I'm going to use that to parlay into a real bite on Brentwood. Then we can go to South America and forget this whole rotten mess.
In the meantime I'm taking pictures of what I'll call a drinking orgy participated in by the police. I'll leave it to you to smuggle a camera in to me and to keep booth thirteen

out of action so I can have it for a stakeout.

When I get finished with those guys, they'll see who the smart one really is.

The letter was signed "Star," and had a six-pointed star consisting of interlaced triangles drawn after the signature.

"That's Starman Calvert's handwriting?" Sellers asked.

She nodded.

"He know anything about *this* apartment?" Sellers went on ruthlessly.

"Don't be so naïve about women," Bertha said. "Take a look at her."

Babe was looking from one to the other like a trapped animal.

Bertha said, "Some women sell themselves to the highest bidder. Others are peddlers. This little tramp is a peddler."

Sergeant Sellers started to say, "We have to be sure that—"

But Bertha, moving forward with slow menace, interposed, "Am I right, dearie?"

"I had to look out for myself," Babe said, cringing back from Bertha's approach.

"Did Starman know anything about *this* apartment?" Bertha asked.

"No! No! You leave me alone!" Babe shouted. "Of course he didn't know anything about this."

"Get your clothes on," Sellers said. "We're going places."

I started for the door.

"Now, where the hell do you think you're going?" Bertha asked.

"You're still under arrest," Sellers told me.

"The hell I am. Here's your case all done up in cellophane and on a silver platter. You want me to gift wrap it as well?"

Sellers thought for a moment, then suddenly said, "I get it now, Pint Size. Go ahead."

"Go where?" Bertha asked.

Sellers grinned. "Don't be so naïve about men, Bertha. He's got unfinished business in Mexico."

Chapter 20

The moon was silvery and tropical. The bay of Todos Santos stirred with the faint whisperings of water on sand.

Lois said, "I wondered if you would come back, Donald—that is, after everything was settled."

"You thought everything would be settled?" I asked.

"I knew you'd work it out *some* way."

"I couldn't have worked it out if I hadn't had you as my ace in the hole. Most girls would have weakened under the pressure. You were one in a thousand, one in a million. You—"

She placed a gentle forefinger over my lips. "I like to hear you say it, Donald, but let's quit talking about murders. How long since you've had any sleep?"

We were lying there on the sand, the moonlight casting long grotesque shadows, the tropical air pulsing with some hidden message which stirred my blood. There wasn't a breath of air stirring. The night was warm and velvety. The moonlight turned the crests of the little, rippling waves to burnished gold. The noise of the wavelets on warm sand was seductive.

I said, "We've got to go back tomorrow, Lois."

She put her arm under my neck, drew my head over to her shoulder.

"That's tomorrow," she said.

There were some questions I had to ask her, some loose threads that I had to tie up, but at the moment I couldn't think of them.

We'd have a long drive back tomorrow. I could think of them then, but as Lois had said, that was tomorrow.